Praise for the Novels
of Eileen Davidson

"The Young and the Restless star Davidson's heroine has an engaging voice laced with humor and irony . . . one need not be a soap fan to enjoy the well-plotted, suspenseful story."
—Romantic Times on
Death In Daytime

"The author's breezy writing style really makes the whole caper fun, without going over the top.
—CA Reviews on
Death In Daytime

"This is a winning series that makes for a perfect companion to the beach . . ."
—Mysterious Reviews on
Dial Emmy For Murder

"Davidson's experience in the field have helped color her books and make them fun and realistic . . ."
—Armchair Review on
Dial Emmy For Murder

"I can't wait for Alexis's further adventures because in true soap opera style, Ms. Davidson ends *Diva Las Vegas* with a cliffhanger, making me yearn for the next mystery."
—TwoLips Reviews on
Diva Las Vegas

". . . fans of the soap opera amateur sleuth series will enjoy this jocular entry because it takes a talented writer to create a work like this."
—Harriett Klausner on
Diva Las Vegas

Also by Eileen Davidson

Death In Daytime

Dial Emmy For Murder

Diva Las Vegas

Eileen Davidson

Swingin' in the Rain

A SOAP OPERA MYSTERY

MIND OVER MATTER BOOKS

ISBN13: 978-0-615-50075-1
ISBN10: 0-615-50075-7

To my sister Mary Elizabeth Davidson,
I'm glad you've got my back.

Chapter 1

"Owww! Your heel's in my ear!" Wes yelled.

"I can't get any traction." My Herve' Leger dress, or rather what was left of it, was in danger of slipping off my body completely. I placed my stilettos on Wes' shoulders. Now I was straddling him.

"Don't look up, Wes!"

"Like I could see anything if I did!" He was right. Rain was pelting us from all sides and flashes of canned lightening were piercing the black sky. I tried again to inch my way up the muddy and very slippery hillside. I felt my pointy-toed Jimmy Choo slide off his shoulders and whack something protruding from his face. Uh oh. His nose?

"Holy Crap!" Wes pulled away in pain, jerking himself out from his position under me. Suddenly I was careening downward.

"AHHHHHHHHH!" I was gathering speed and had no way of stopping. Mud was flying everywhere. A big plop of wet goo landed in my eyes and in my nostrils making me gasp for air. I felt my shoe heel hook onto what I assumed was a cable that connected the lights at the top of the hill to the electrical truck at the bottom. I now had a collection of lights and their metal stands trailing behind me. I wiped the mud from my right eye and looked behind just in time to see them gaining on me.

"Oh, nooooo," I cried. Just then someone grabbed my arm and jerked me out of the path of the plummeting lights, to safety. It was the director, Sandy.

"Cut! Turn off the rain!" she yelled. Then added dryly, "You missed your mark again, Alex." The lights had swept past us and landed in a pile at the bottom of the hill.

"Gee thanks, Sandy, for being so sensitive." I spat out some grass and dirt.

"I got you out of the way, didn't I?" she asked as she turned to the special effects guys. "I said turn off the rain, damn it!"

"It *is* off, Sandy! It's real rain. From the sky rain," Wes answered covering his nose. He's a stage hand I've known forever and a real salt of the earth kind of guy. Most crew people are.

Jennifer from wardrobe came running over shielding me with an umbrella.

"We've got to get these prepped in case we have to do another take." She took my shoes and gave me galoshes.

"Thanks, Jen!" I yelled as she ran off to the wardrobe trailer.

"You okay, Alex?" Patti asked covering me with a towel. She was rubbing her hands together to stay warm and I noticed something on one of her wrists.

"You're a party girl." Patti looked puzzled and I pointed to her wrist. The residual imprint of a fleur-de-lis was still visible on her skin. It looked like what was left of a stamp. You know, the kind they give you at a nightclub that you can't get off for weeks on end no matter how hard you scrub? "Clubbing last night?" I asked. Patti quickly put her hand in her coat pocket. "I'm impressed! I rarely stay up past nine!"

"Let's get you dry, huh? Too bad you didn't get hit by the lighting equipment cuz then we'd all have to go home, ya know?"

I *was* impressed by Patti's clubbing. She had to be pushing 60. She's been in the make-up department on our soap opera "The Bare and the Brazen" for 30 years and has seen it all. She's a true professional and I had rarely heard her complain. I guess these adverse working conditions were even getting to her. She smiled wearily and wiped some mud from my mouth with a tissue.

"Yechh! What the hell are we doing here, anyway, huh? This sucks."

That was a good question. "The Bare and the Brazen's" ratings had been slipping the last few years, along with all the other soaps. Another soap, "The Depths of the Sea" had already been cancelled last year so The Powers That Be decided, in an attempt to bring the ratings up, and avoid cancellation completely, that we'd go on "location" for a few episodes. I use the term "location" loosely. We were in Griffith Park, about fifteen minutes from the studio. It was 4:30a.m. and we'd been there since 6:00p.m. the previous night. Gone were the days when we'd go to Hawaii or Paris for a week on a location shoot. Budget issues had relegated us to a park or sometimes even the studio parking lot. To make matters even worse, Southern California was in the grip of the worst El Nino in decades. For all you who are unfamiliar with what El Nino is, it's a Spanish name for "Lots of Fucking Rain," or "disruption of the ocean-atmosphere system in the tropical Pacific" that messes with the weather, bringing torrential rains for weeks upon weeks.

I looked over and saw my victim, Wes, pulling cable. One hand covered a bloody nose.

"Sorry, Wes. I couldn't help it. Did I break your nose?"

"Nah. I'm okay." He took a few steps and turned back smiling. "And I didn't look up your dress. Not that I wasn't tempted."

"Yeah, sure you were." I smacked him on the back. "Thanks for taking so much abuse. You think we got the shot? Please don't tell me we have to do this again."

Sandy walked up just in time to hear me.

"Of course we have to do it again. I told you. You missed your mark!" Sandy said pulling a twig from behind my ear.

"At least we don't need the rain truck anymore, right?" I asked hopefully. I mean, why would we need fake rain when we were in the middle of an ongoing never-ending deluge. Sandy looked at me with something that resembled compassion.

"This rain," she said gesturing towards the sky, "doesn't look real. We need the fake rain because it looks more real than the real rain." She said this with a straight face. Only in Hollywood.

"We have to hurry. The sun will be coming up very soon." She slogged off yelling, "Reset the lightening and rain to number one and let's do it again. Quickly! We're losing the night."

"She's losing the night and I'm losing my mind," I muttered to myself as I headed to the hair and make-up trailer.

Chapter 2

I climbed the stairs to the "honey wagon". (These are trailers and/or trucks set up for hair and make-up and everything else you might need on location. The name "honey" wagon was coined eons ago in reference to portable latrines. Someone had a sense of humor!) Thank God it was nice and warm in there. I shook my umbrella off and unwrapped the towels that had been wrapped around me. Then I looked in the mirror and screamed.

"Oh my God!" My hair had grass and mud in it and my mascara had completely run down my face, I looked like "Alice Cooper: The Early Years." George, my best friend and hairdresser, stomped into the trailer behind me. His wet hair was plastered to his head and he had a steady stream of water dripping off his nose. He didn't look like he was having any fun at all. He held a brush in his hand but I wasn't sure if he was going to try to do something with my hair, or smack me with it. Granted he was only 5'4" but he could still be intimidating.

"I can't go on camera like this. Do something." I sat down in the hair chair in front of him. He looked mad

"Please?"

"I thought you were a method actress. Don't you want realism?" He was definitely mad at me.

"Realism is one thing. This . . . ," I gestured to the mirror, ". . . is too real."

"Fine." And he started combing through my rat's nest, head of hair.

"Excuse me. What did I do?" I asked him.

"It's what you didn't do. You have to get up the hill and hit your mark! I wanna go home!" He tossed a make-up sponge at me.

It's not my fault that we're here at all! It's Felicia's fault!" I said as I took the sponge and started removing the rivulets of mascara from my face.

We were here in these horrible conditions because the character I played, Felicia, had amnesia. She had lost her memory after discovering that the man she had always thought was her father, was not. Her biological father was actually a golf pro her mother had had an affair with back in the day. She couldn't handle the trauma and had developed amnesia, causing her to leave her mansion and wander off into the hills. During the night. In a rainstorm. Did I mention she was wearing a very short white "bandage" dress when this occurred?

"That's why you get paid the big bucks, Missy! C'mon! You can do it! What do you think?" I looked in the mirror and although it wasn't my finest hour, it would have to do. I got up and George pushed me, prodding me forward with his brush.

"The bucks are not *that* big anymore. By the way, I get it. I want to go home, too," I said swatting at him. "You're not the only one who has a nice warm boyfriend waiting for you in bed, ya know."

George stopped abruptly. "Oops! I forgot to tell you. Jakes called on your cell while you were *not* hitting your mark."

"Is it Sarah?" I asked, alarmed. Sarah is my seven-year-old daughter.

Jakes was watching her that night and it was 4 a.m.

"No, no it's not Sarah. I would have remembered that. But he did say it was important." I whacked him on the head. "Sorry. I'll go get your phone." George walked to the front of the trailer.

Jakes is my boyfriend. My handsome, hunky, police detective boyfriend.

"Alex! We need you on set. We're ready to go!" Herbie, our stage manager, poked his head into the trailer.

"I gotta make a call, Herbie."

"We gotta go *now*, Al. If we don't, we won't get the shot." He gestured out the door.

I took a peek and saw the beginnings of morning light over the horizon and I could sense panic developing on the set. If we didn't get this shot before the sun came up it could end up costing Production literally thousands and thousands of dollars. All of this torture would have been for nothing. Now it was all on me.

"Okay, let's go," I said as I descended the trailer steps. A torrent of rain hit me square in the face. Herbie grabbed the umbrella and held it over my head. "You're sure it wasn't Sarah, George?" I yelled, trying to avoid the wet.

"I'm positive. I asked Jakes if it was and he said no." George yelled, running after me and handing me my cell phone. Jennifer was next to join us, giving me the now fairly clean and dry Jimmy Choo shoes.

"Oh good, you cleaned up your mascara. I was going to do that on set," Patti said as she caught up to us.

We were all drenched as we found our way back to the bottom of the hill. Wes was waiting for me, clearly a glutton for punishment. I took off my boots and put on my shoes, adjusted myself as Sandy hollered,

"Let's go, everyone. The sun is coming up. This is it! We have one shot at this! Start the rain! Alex get ready to climb. And hit your mark!"

It had already been raining but now it was a monsoon. I could barely see in front of myself when I heard Herbie yell out, "Alex. Your cell phone!" Stupid me. I still had my phone in my hand.

"Oh Geez!" I quickly glanced down and saw a text from Jakes. It said: "Call me URGENT Randy's dead." I stopped in my tracks. Randy? My creepy ex-husband and father to my child, dead? Herbie grabbed the phone from me and jumped out of the way.

"Action!"

Chapter 3

"Are you sure you're ready for this?" Jakes asked.

The answer was no, I wasn't. Granted, my ex, Randy, had not been my favorite person. Primarily because he cleaned out our bank accounts and left the country then came back without having to spend a single day in jail. On top of that he recently had the nerve to petition for joint custody of our daughter. But that didn't mean I wanted to see him dead. Okay, I *had* wished him dead. Many times. Maybe I was feeling more than a little guilty that my wish had come true.

We were standing in a hallway just outside the autopsy room. The smell of chemicals seemed to ooze from the walls. I guess that was better than the smell of death. I was still freezing from being out all night in the rain but that was nothing compared to the cold that assaulted me when Jakes pushed the door open. A body was lying on a metal table with a white sheet covering it. I gasped.

"I'm sorry, Alex," Jakes said, "you're the closest thing to a relative we have. We need somebody to positively I.D. him—"

"I know, I know," I said, with more confidence than I felt. "It's okay. I can do this." I grabbed his arm and held tightly as we walked inside.

The room was large and spacious, but not dimly lit and moody like in the *CSI* shows. It was blindingly bright and very sterile. I couldn't bring myself to look at the table just yet so I glanced around the room instead. It was fascinating. Albeit morbidly so. Pretty much empty, except for the body, a large scale hung from the ceiling directly over the table. For organs, I assumed. Ugh. I almost threw up in my mouth at the thought of that one. There were jars and vials on shelves. Cupboards with glass doors held various files and chemicals. I saw another smaller office to the right side. The faint glow of a television could be seen from under the closed door. I thought there was something vaguely familiar about the voice I heard coming from in there. Just when I didn't think it could get any more surreal a very large man in a white coat came bursting out of the office.

"Why hello, there. Ms. Peterson! I heard it was you coming in. So happy to meet you." His voice was booming as if he was doing Shakespeare. Shakespeare in the morgue. He grabbed my hand and pumped it, determined to cause me bodily harm. "I'm Dr. Willis. Or rather, Richard."

With the door left open I could see what was playing on the plasma screen behind him. It was me. Yikes.

"I was just watching you, or rather, Felicia on my TIVO. She's really losing it, isn't she? Ha ha." He took his glasses out of his lab coat pocket and put them on. Stepping back he gave me a once over. "You look much taller on T.V." He got a little closer to me. He smelled like peppermint. Sucking on the end of his glasses he asked, "Tell me, as an actor, do you find it more rewarding to play the heroine or the villain? I imagine each has its own rewards."

I looked to Jakes and gave him a "what the . . ." look.

"Ms. Peterson has had a very long night. Maybe we could get on with the I.D.?"

Dr. Willis pursed his lips for a moment, squinted his eyes and looked at me. He abruptly turned to the table with the body on it and picked up a clipboard, suddenly all business.

"Could you please come over to the table, Ms. Peterson? What, or rather, who do we have here? I understand this poor soul could be your ex-husband? A Mr. Randall Moore?"

I made my way over next to the table. Jakes stood behind me, as if preparing to hold me up.

"Ready?" Jakes asked as he held my hand tightly. "This could be rough."

"No, I'll be fine." How bad could it be, right? I had seen dead people before, after all.

Dr. Willis pulled the sheet down to mid-chest and my stomach dropped. Randy's face was slightly distorted but strangely, even in death, He was still handsome. I felt a sudden rush of affection for him. There he was, my daughter's father. I had loved him once.

I couldn't stop looking at him. I heard the doctor clear his throat. "Sorry, that is, umm, that's Randy," I said.

"Okay," Jakes said to Dr Willis, but didn't even wait for him to cover Randy again. He hustled me out of there and onto a chair in the hall. Dr. Willis followed.

"Ms. Peterson, are you okay? Would you like some water?"

"I'm fine, thank you, Doctor," I managed to say.

"Well, it was a pleasure to meet you." He looked at me for a moment longer. Oh God, was he actually going to ask for an autograph? He must have thought better of it because he turned and quickly went back into the room, closing the door behind him.

"*Would* you like some water?" Jakes asked wrapping me in his arms and gently kissing me on the forehead.

"What I want is a good stiff drink."

"Really?" He glanced at his watch. "It's only ten in the morning."

"Really."

He obliged.

Chapter 4

Jakes took me to a nearby bar. He rarely took me to cop hangouts, but it was obvious as we walked to a back booth that this was a favorite. Even at 10 in the a.m. police types were everywhere.

We took off our raincoats and hung them up. I knew I looked like a drowned rat, especially after the night's shooting, but it didn't matter much at the moment. A waitress came over and I ordered a Maker's Mark, neat with a chaser of French fries. Jakes just ordered coffee.

I put my head in my hands, my elbows on the table. I couldn't bring myself to ask how Randy had died. So I asked about our daughter, instead.

"What am I going to tell Sarah?"

Jakes had volunteered to watch Sarah for me when I found out I had to pull an all nighter for the show. Even though he was supposed to be off duty, we knew that that could change in an instant. Thankfully, I alerted my neighbor, Tonja, that we might need her in case of an emergency. My mom lives with us and is my "nanny" but she was visiting our relatives back home in the Midwest.

"Sometimes it takes a village. Seriously. Thank God for Tonja." I said.

Jakes picked up a napkin and wiped some mud from the side of my face. "I called her earlier. She said she got Sarah off to school."

I kissed him gently on the lips. It felt so good to be close to a warm, and living, being. "Thank God for you."

"Yeah. What a night."

"You haven't heard the least of it!"

The waitress brought our drinks and a basket of fries. I started in on my breakfast of champions and began to tell about the night from hell. The freezing rain and anal retentive director. How we had managed to get the last scene, even after the "Randy's dead" text, and thankfully, before the sun came up.

Jakes looked at me and nodded. He knew I had been avoiding the question.

"Okay," I said, now that I had the drink in my hand and had taken a good, healthy swallow, "what happened?"

"All we know," Jakes said, "is that he was found at the bottom of a mud slide."

"A mud slide. How random is that?" I shook my head. I couldn't believe I was actually having this conversation. "Was he already dead?"

"Very."

"Mud slide where?"

"At the house he was renting in The Palisades. It was situated at the top of a hill. We're just assuming at this point, that he'd been washed down the hill."

"Did the house slide down with Randy in it?" It sounded very strange, I know, but this happened many more times in rain ravaged Southern California than you would imagine.

"No. Just him. We don't know for sure what killed him, though," Jakes said. "It could have been the fall, he could have suffocated in the mud. There's still going to have to be an autopsy."

I took another sip, felt it burn its way down my throat and popped a handful of greasy fries in my mouth. The thought of telling Sarah that her daddy was dead was upsetting me more than Randy actually being dead. I hate to sound crass but, realistically speaking, him being gone solved a lot of problems for me.

"When will the autopsy results be in?" I asked.

"Probably tomorrow morning."

"Do you have any idea when this happened?" I asked. "How long he was lying there?"

"I went to the scene," he said. "It must have happened in the middle of last night, around one or two. The neighbor below him heard the slide as it was happening and called nine-one-one. Fire trucks and a couple of squad cars responded. One of the cops saw a leg sticking out of the mud. Pulled the poor guy out. Luckily, he hadn't fallen all the way to PCH. Not that it would have mattered. Dead is dead. That's when they called me."

"Wait a minute," I said. "Why did they call you? You're a homicide detective. This wasn't a homicide—was it?"

"The cop who pulled Randy out of the mud was the same cop I used a couple of years ago to follow him. Remember we thought he was stalking you?" I nodded. "He kept a picture of Randy on hand for months. When he turned him over and saw his face last night he immediately recognized him. He called me right away."

I tossed a few more fries in my mouth and rubbed my hands together.

"I'm still so cold. I can't get my hands warm."

He took both my hands in his. They were warm and comforting. We sat like that for quite a while.

Chapter 5

Jakes wanted to follow me home in his car.

"You're upset, and you've had a drink," was his reasoning.

"I really only had two sips. Whiskey in the morning doesn't do it for me. At least we know I'm not an alcoholic, right?" I was trying to be glib, but Jakes saw right through me. "I'll be okay. I just really want to get out of these wet clothes, and have a talk with Sarah."

"Are you sure you shouldn't wait until you have more facts?"

"The only fact that Sarah will be concerned with," I started tearing up, "is that she's never going to see her daddy again. She just spent last Saturday with him, and she came home so happy."

How could I have done that to her? Randy had convinced me it was the best thing, to let her get to know her father again. Even after everything he had done to us, I knew he loved his little girl and I wanted that for her. I had relented and was okay with her seeing him on occasion. But not joint custody. Even now I became incensed at the thought of him filing and a judge even considering it. Now I was kicking myself for ever allowing him even one day with her.

How was I going tell her she'd lost her father? Again?

Jakes and I walked to my car, sharing an umbrella and gingerly avoiding puddles.

"You be careful on the roads, okay? There's a lot of sigalerts out there." He opened the door for me and I got in. The rain was starting to really come down now and I felt like I had to shout to be heard.

"I will. You, too. What time will you be over?"

"I'll call you. Drive slowly!" He kissed me, closed the umbrella and tossed it in the back of the car and ran off in the direction of his car.

I looked out the window at the sheets of relentless rain. I had gotten my way and began to drive home without an escort. Probably not the smartest move considering the condition of the freeway. Traffic was stop and go as people tried to avoid flooded patches all the way down the 10.

Cars were skidding out. Stalled cars littered the side of the freeway. It was like being in a video game.

It took over two hours to drive through that mess. It usually takes 30 minutes. I felt like I'd been through a war and was so relieved to get home. I ran into my 1920's Craftsman style house, stripping off my wet and dirty clothes. In the laundry room, looking out the back window, I could see the canal had risen and was starting to flood over our dock. Oh great. Even the ducks, usually floating serenely by, had paddled for cover. This was just what I needed. Noah's Ark.

The weather fit my mood and I sat down on my sofa and cried. Not because I would miss Randy. He was a pain in the ass. But we had been married, we loved each other at one time, and most importantly, he was Sarah's father.

I still had two hours before I had to get Sarah so I took a much needed hot shower. I must have washed my face ten times so my extraordinarily astute seven year old daughter wouldn't ask me what I had been crying about. I threw on some sweats and was heading out the door when the phone rang. It was my neighbor, Tonja.

Tonja is in her thirties and going through a divorce. She was trying to get her life back on track, working part time as a computer programmer for various small businesses in Venice and Santa Monica. She had moved in a month ago and watched Sarah on occasion, for some extra cash. She was good with kids, outgoing and friendly.

"Hey Tonja. Thank you so much for taking care of Sarah last night. I hope it wasn't too much of an inconvenience."

"No problemo. I just bundled up and came on over. We crashed on your sofa. I hope that's okay?"

"Of course. Whatever. I owe you."

"Yes. You do! Now maybe we can have that drink you've been promising?" Tonja had been trying to get me to go out for a drink since she had moved in, but with work and Sarah and Jakes, I hadn't managed to make the time.

"You're on." I checked the clock on the mantle. "Hey, look, I have to get Sarah."

"Do you want me to come by when she's home? I promised to teach her some cheerleading moves after school today."

Tonja had been a Laker's cheerleader in the 90's and had the body to show it. She was quite the dichotomy. Killer brain and a killer bod.

"So, what was going on with Jakes? He had an emergency, huh? He ran out of here so fast."

"I gotta get going. We'll catch up later, okay? Thanks again!" That was the last thing I wanted to get into. I hung up and headed out to my car. Now my cell phone rang.

It was Connie, my ex-manager.

"Hi Doll. I just heard about Randy. How you holding up?" Hearing her signature gravelly voice was actually a comfort.

"Hi, Con. I'm okay. Thanks for calling. It's pretty weird," I answered as I drove to Sarah's school.

"How's Sarah doing? Does she know, yet?"

"No, I haven't told her. And I don't know how she'll take it." There was an awkward pause.

"Well, don't let her watch or listen to the news until you do. Anyway, you know where I am if you need me, right Al? Still there for ya."

"Thanks, Connie. And thanks for calling." She hung up and I felt a little more than wistful.

Connie had been my manager for quite a few years. The projects she wanted me to take were dubious at best. I had decided to fire her when she started pressuring me to go on *Rehabbing with the Stars*. Especially since I didn't have an addiction to go to rehab for. "But they pay a hundred thousand dollars! And I've seen the wine you go through. Seriously, maybe you need a little re-evaluation." I knew then it was time to part ways. I couldn't, in good conscience, go to rehab for an addiction to two glasses of Merlot a night. No matter how much they paid. Connie was, well Connie. She's a little nutty with questionable judgment but she was my friend. And I couldn't help but feel the loss of yet another relationship.

I felt a sudden sense of urgency to see my little girl as I pulled up in front of her school.

"Guess what Tonja and I did this morning, Mom? It was so cool!" Sarah said as dropped her backpack on the kitchen table. "She made pancakes and I made scrambled eggs! And they were so good, too. She knows how to make fancy food. Like apple pie, and guess what? She knows how to do back flips. She said she'll teach me. I think I want to be a cheerleader, too."

"Honey, I need to talk to you." I sat down. "Come sit with me."

"Wait, Mom. Wait, okay? I promised I'd draw Tonja a picture and I want to do it before I forget." She skipped down the hall to her room. She was so happy I didn't want to ruin it. I decided to let her have a little time.

Maybe I'd make some cocoa first before I tell her anything. Maybe I'd call someone for advice.

Someone like George.

Chapter 6

"What was the emergency, honey?" he asked. "Is Sarah okay?"

I had left the set the night before, telling everyone I had a "family emergency."

"Oh George," I said, keeping my voice down, "you won't believe it. Randy's dead."

"OMG! How?"

"Mud slide." There was a long pause.

"Mud slide? Death by mud slide? Seriously?" He hesitated a long time then said, tentatively, "Well, that's not really *bad* news, is it? I mean, considering?"

"I wanted him out of our lives," I said, "but I never wanted him dead."

"Yeah, you did," he reminded me quickly. "When he first took off you said you wanted to kill him—"

"Yes," I said, interrupting him, "that was a long time ago. I was angry and hurt."

"And again when you thought he was trying to drive you off of PCH and kill you. Remember?"

"Okay, I know. I know! I wanted him dead. And I don't feel good about it," I said. "So now he really is dead. And he was Sarah's dad, for pete's sake. Now I have to tell her."

"Well, she didn't really know him. I mean hadn't she just spent a day or two with him since she was two or three years old?" he asked.

"George. I called you for some compassion and some advice. She's a little girl who lost her daddy. Twice! It's still going to hurt."

"You're right," he said. "That was insensitive of me. It's just hard to feel sad about Randy. He was a prick. Sorry. When are you going to tell her?"

"After dinner, I think. I mean, I'm going to try . . ."

"Well, I think you should wait. Have you slept yet today?"

I hadn't. Wow. I was really tired.

"No. And I'm pretty pooped."

"I think you should get some sleep. No sleep, no decisions. Call me if you need to talk some more. I want to hear everything. Mud slide?" he said. "Someone's beeping in. It's the studio. Are you coming in tomorrow?"

"Yeah. I'm in. I don't know what time, yet. Love you."

"Love you. Talk to you later."

I hung up and started to make some hot cocoa when the phone rang. I saw on the caller I.D. that it was Jakes.

"You got word already?"

"No," he said. "Can you talk?"

"Not really."

"Then just listen. The autopsy hasn't been done yet, but the M.E. has determined the probable cause of death."

"And?"

"Alex, Randy was murdered."

"What?"

"And that's not all," he said. "You're the ex-spouse, Alex. The ex-spouse who had been abandoned, had her money stolen, and was in a custody case with the victim. Baby, that makes you the number one suspect."

"You've got to be kidding me," I dropped the spoon in the saucepan. "That's the most ridiculous thing I've ever heard."

"Well, you can understand why you'd be considered, can't you? You're in an ugly custody fight." Jakes said.

"That's just stupid. If every ex who was in an ugly custody battle killed their former spouse, Los Angeles would be a ghost town."

"True. But he did leave you in debt when he took your savings and left the country."

Randy was dead, God bless him, but what an asshole! He was the gift that kept on giving. "Okay. So . . ." I took a deep breath and tried to regain my composure. ". . . all I have to do is tell them where I was when Randy was murdered, right? That'll clear me. When was he killed?"

"We're not sure yet. The thing is, Alex . . . I called to let you know that they want to bring you in for questioning."

"What? Oh my God. Not again." I had gone through this a couple of years ago when I had been a suspect in another murder. *The Yearning Tide's* head writer had been bludgeoned to death with her Emmy. It was common knowledge she hadn't liked me much, so many assumed I was responsible. That's how Jake's and I had met.

"When do they want to see me?" I peeked around the corner and saw that Sarah was still in her room.

"This evening."

"What? They can't. What will I do . . ."

"It's okay. I handled it. I think it's just a formality, Babe. Really. I told them you'd come in on your own in the next twenty-four hours. When can you make it in?"

I reached over to the table where my script was and looked at the next day's shooting schedule. I was in early and out early. "I can make it to the station around eleven or twelve."

"I'll tell them you'll be there at noon." Jakes knew me well enough to know this wasn't just a formality for me. I already felt I was defending my life . . . again.

Chapter 7

I was definitely preoccupied as I drove onto the studio lot. Have you ever experienced those weird time lapses when you can't remember how you got somewhere? You're just here and then you're there and don't recall anything in between? That was me that morning.

I had dropped Sarah off at school and the next thing I knew I was pulling into the WBN parking lot. I decided not to tell her about her father just yet. There were some things I needed to sort out first, like whether or not I was going to be arrested for murder. I hadn't slept after the conversation with Jakes the previous night. He ended up having to work late so he didn't come over. He was better off, considering I tossed and turned all night. Now that was two nights in a row with no sleep. Today wasn't going to be easy.

I drove around and around the parking lot, looking for a space. For the last two years *American Popstar* had been using one of the stages at the studio to film their show. This meant that parking spaces were few and far between. I wasn't in the mood so I called the Production Office of *The Bare and the Brazen* for help.

"Hey, Erin. No parking *again*." I sounded grumpy. Especially compared to Erin, who was our perpetually bubbly Production Assistant. "Good morning, Gorgeous Woman! I'll call Security and see where you can park. Wait a sec." She put me on hold as I put my car in park and waited. I stared through my windshield; the *thwack thwack thwack* of the wipers put me in a hypnotic trance. More rain. Then I saw something red out of the corner of my eye that got my attention. There was someone on the balcony outside the stage door, holding a bright red umbrella. This wouldn't have been that odd except for the fact that it was still pouring rain.

The balcony was about 50 yards away from me and on the second floor. I could see that it was Patti, my make-up artist. She was hunkered under the umbrella, talking on her cell phone very animatedly. She was too far away to see for sure but it certainly looked like she was crying. I was trying to get a closer look when my phone beeped. It was call waiting from Herbie, our Stage Manager. I was about to get it when Erin's voice came back on the line.

"Okay, Sweetie," she exclaimed like it was the best news ever, "Security says for you to park on the upper lot in guest parking. There are cones up there blocking the spots but just remove one and it's yours!"

"Thanks, Erin."

The upper lot was a considerable distance away from The Artists' Entrance, or front door to the studio. I was going to get wet. I put the car in drive.

I found a space, got out and moved the cone. Even though I ran back to my car, I was drenched. "Damn *American Popstar!*" I muttered. I grabbed my bag and umbrella and made a beeline for the studio, completely forgetting to check my voicemail. My phone was ringing as I peeled off my sopping coat and dropped it on the sofa in my dressing room.

"Yeah?"

"Come on up. We need to get you ready, fast. Priscilla called in sick so you're up first." George's voice was frantic.

"I'm on my way." I hung up. "Crap! That's what Herbie wanted!" I ran to the closet, stripped off my street clothes and threw on the cashmere sweater dress Jennifer had pulled for me. I yanked on black tights and black leather boots. Then I grabbed the gold hoop earrings that were lying on the counter and headed up to hair and make- up.

"She's here! She's here!" George was saying into the phone. He hung up. "That was Herbie. We have about ten minutes to get you camera ready. Sit!"

"What is this craziness?" I asked George as I sat in front of him.

"Oh my God. You have no idea. All hell's breaking loose today. Priscilla is sick first of all. And we just found out that *The Best Days are Ahead* and *The Tears of Tomorrow* have been cancelled!"

"What? Why?" That was really bad news. That only left four soaps on the air. This day was just getting better.

"I guess the network is replacing them with a cooking show and a talk

show. Like we don't have enough of those on the air. And not just that. . ."
George bent down and got close to my ear. "Patti is having a breakdown.
She got a phone call and I swear she started freaking out. She had to leave
the room." He twisted my hair and stuck a pin in it.

"Ow! Careful! I saw her out on the balcony before I came in. I thought
she was crying and it looked like she was in an argument or something."
I was concerned on many different levels. "Where is she, now? And more
importantly, who's going to do my make-up?" I hated to sound self-serv-
ing, but the show must go on. Or at least that's what everyone has told
me.

"Alex. We need you in five. Five minutes, Alex." Herbie's voice came
booming over the PA system.

"Marlene?" George yelled over to another make-up artist whose chair
was next to Patti's. "Can you take Alex? Like right now?" Marlene put
down the file she was using on her nails and slowly got up from her chair.
She was a vision in orange. It was Marlene's favorite color and she wore
a variation of oranges and tangerine tones every day. Even her hair had
those overtones. The color definitely complimented her beautiful cocoa
colored skin. Interesting because orange is a very vibrant and exciting col-
or and Marlene had a very laid-back personality. She didn't let anything
ruffle her tail feathers. Not even a stressful situation like getting an actress
ready in five minutes.

"Sure thing," Marlene drawled in a voice that was like honey on a hot
biscuit. "Come on over here, Alex. We'll get you fixed up."

George put the last hairpin into my chignon and I scooted over to
Marlene's chair.

"Thanks, Marlene. You know what Patti uses on me right?" I asked as
I looked over my lines for my first scene. I glanced up just in time to see
Marlene rolled her eyes. "Sorry, I know this isn't your first rodeo." I let
Marlene do her thing, as I tried to remember my lines. She got me done in
record time.

"You nailed it. Thanks!" I hopped out of her chair just as I heard, "Alex
to set, please. Alex?" over the PA.

"Talk about timing! Follow me down to set." George said. As we got
outside the hair and make-up room he added, "How'd it go with Sarah,
any way? Is she okay?"

"I took your advice and I didn't tell her. I've got some big news,
George." We were nearing the bottom of the stairs. "The police want to
question me about Randy's death."

George stopped suddenly and turned around to face me. "Listen to this." He got very close to me. "When Patti was on the phone? I heard her say something like 'I could get there by eleven.' She hung up and ran out of the room so upset I felt I just had to check the caller I.D. You'll never guess what it said." He glanced around making sure no one was in earshot. "It said Los Angeles Police Department."

"Why would they want to see Patti?" Just then Herbie walked over and looked at me impatiently. "Sorry, Herbie. I'm there."

If I thought this day was going to be tough earlier, I had no idea what lay ahead.

Chapter 8

I taped my scenes for the day, and since there was a little time to kill before I had to go downtown, I wandered back upstairs to the make-up room to sniff around. Patti was still MIA. In fact the whole room looked deserted.

"You looking for Patti?" I jumped. It was Ralph, another make-up artist stationed in the corner. Before I could answer, he volunteered, "Everyone's at a production meeting because of that snafu at the remote. We have to re-shoot, you know."

"Yeah, I heard. That's a drag, huh?" I went over to Patti's station and pretended to be fixing my make-up. I don't know what I was hoping to find, if anything. My instincts told me the LAPD thing was not a coincidence. I opened a drawer and something caught my eye. It was a napkin with a logo on it. Where had I seen that before? Then I remembered. It was the same one I'd seen on Patti's wrist at the remote. "Trois ou Plus" it read. And an address. A club I'd never heard of. Not unusual since I didn't go out much. My cell rang and it was Jakes.

"You done?" he asked me.

"Yeah, in fact I'm leaving now. I'll see you in twenty." I disconnected the call. "Bye Ralph, have a nice day!"

"See ya, Alex!" And he got back to his magazine.

The new Headquarters was at 100 W. First Street, which had replaced the old Parker Center. I hadn't been to the new Headquarters yet, but Jakes was waiting just inside the door, in the lobby, to accompany me to the proper floor.

"How are you liking the new building?" I asked in the elevator. I was nervous and just wanted to make conversation.

"The cafeteria still needs work," he said. "Aside from that, it's an architectural nightmare."

We got off on the Robbery Homicide floor and he walked me to the Homicide Section. It reminded me of the old building, just cleaner floors, walls and desks. Even the holding cages were clean.

Jakes walked me to his desk and said, "Wait here. I'll let the detective in charge know you're here."

"I wish you were the detective in charge." I must have looked a little scared because he put his arm around me.

"You'll do fine, baby," he said. "I can't be, because of our relationship."

As he walked away I thought how silly it was for me to be nervous. I knew I was innocent, so what was the big deal? Maybe because when I had been in this situation before, so many people had believed I could be a killer. It made me nervous realizing how easily people rush to judgment.

Jakes came back with a man I had never seen before. He was tall—not as tall as Jakes, though—slender, in his late thirties. And he was clean. I mean, he seemed fastidious about it. Hair short and perfect, suit impeccable, tie just right, shoes shined.

"Alex Peterson, this is Detective Sam Rockland."

"Miss Peterson," Detective Rockland said, shaking my hand. "I'm sorry for your loss."

He called me "Miss" which meant he knew Randy was my ex, but it was still polite to show me some sympathy.

"Thank you."

"And thank you for coming in," he said. "I just have a few questions."

I stood up.

"Should we go to an interview room?" I asked.

"That won't be necessary. We can talk at my desk."

He stepped aside and gestured with a folder for me to precede him. I looked at Jakes, who nodded and said, "I'll wait here."

"Okay."

I went ahead and he stopped me when we'd gone about three desks up.

"Right here," he said. The chair simply sat by his desk, but he held the back of it for me, anyway. His manners were as impeccable as the rest of him. His scent lingered while he sat behind his desk. He put the folder down in front of him. On it was written in Sharpi: Randall Moore.

He opened the folder and pulled out a small notebook, clicked his ballpoint pen and looked at me.

"I understand you and your ex-husband were involved in a heated custody battle."

"Well . . . yes." I had been royally pissed off when Randy said he wanted to share custody. I couldn't believe he had the nerve to want to be Sarah's father again after stealing our money, leaving the country and not even having to pay for it. Heated. That was a good word for it.

"When was the last time you saw him?"

"Last weekend."

"Under what circumstances?"

"He came to pick up our daughter to spend the day with her."

"Did he bring her back on time?"

"Um, yes, he did . . . for a change."

"So there have been times when he didn't bring her back promptly."

"Well, yes."

"And how did that make you feel? When he brought her back late?"

How did it make me feel? Terrified? Livid? After all, he took off with our money, was gone for a few years. What was to keep him from taking off with our daughter? And yet, until the final decision, the court had given him one day a week with her.

"Angry?" he asked.

"Yes."

"Scared?"

"Oh, yes."

"How late was he bringing her back?" Rockland asked.

"About an hour."

"So, then, not late enough for you to start looking for him?"

"What do you mean?"

"I mean making calls, to his home, or getting in the car to try and find him?"

"No," I said, "not that late."

"Miss Peterson," her asked, "where were you the night before last?"

"What time?" I asked.

"All night," Rockland said. "I'll make the question easier. Did you see your ex the night before last, at any time?"

"No," I said. "I was working all night on location in Griffith Park."

"Sounds like you have lots of witnesses."

"Yes."

"All day and night?"

"I took my daughter to school in the morning," I said, "ran some errands, and then went to work."

"Errands?"

"I went to the bank, bought some groceries, took my lap top to be fixed, and then went to work."

"I see. And did you pick your daughter up from school in the afternoon?"

"No," I said, "I had to work."

"So, did your ex pick her up, then?"

"No."

"Why not?"

"It wasn't his day," I said.

"Then who did pick her up?"

I paused for a second. I couldn't fathom what any of these questions had to do with Randy being murdered. Was there a method to this? "Detective Jakes did."

"Ah . . ."

"Detective Rockland," I asked, "am I a suspect in my ex-husband's death?"

"A suspect?" he asked. "Did I give you that impression?"

"Sort of." He knew he had.

"Well, I'm sorry, then," Rockland said. "I didn't mean to imply that. I was just asking some routine questions. It's true when a man or woman is killed, the spouse is often the main suspect. But I don't believe that's the case, here. In fact, I don't have any more questions for you."

"That's it?" I asked. "We're finished?"

He nodded and said, "We're finished."

I stood up, still unsure about whether I could leave or not. I was pleased to find out I wasn't a suspect in Randy's death, but was Detective Rockland telling me the truth?

"Thank you," he said. As he stood up he dropped the folder on the ground. I bent over to pick it up. Photos fluttered to the floor. Dead Randy photos at the scene of the mud slide.

"Sorry about that, Miss Peterson." He reached to take them back, but my expression must have gotten his attention.

"Are you all right?"

I shook my head. It was disturbing seeing Randy like that. Then I noticed something when I was handing the photos back. "I never knew Randy had a tattoo." One was clearly visible on the inside of his lower forearm. "He never had one when we were together. He said they were crass."

"Well, I guess he changed his mind." He took the photos and put them back in his folder. "Thanks, again Miss Peterson."

I nodded, and walked back to Jakes' desk.

"All done?" he asked.

"You tell me," I said. I threw a sour look back at Rockland, who didn't notice. "He says I'm not a suspect. Is he telling me the truth?"

"Let's go get some lunch," he said, "and we'll talk about it."

Chapter 9

Lunch was one of those chi chi food trucks that are all the rage. It was a gourmet restaurant on wheels parked just outside the new headquarters. Jakes nodded to the people he knew from the building. We waited in line and didn't start talking until we had our chicken crepes and Café au laits. We claimed a couple of steps in front of the building to sit on.

"Sorry for the quick lunch, but I have to get back inside," he looked at me closely. "Are you okay?"

"Not really. On top of everything else going on I just found out that two more soaps were cancelled. That only leaves four on the air. Can't help thinking soaps are an endangered species." I looked around. The rain had actually stopped; for a change and it was nice to be outside.

"Sorry to hear that. Will *The Bare and the Brazen* be safe?"

"For a while, I guess. We have good ratings. But it's relative now. Our good ratings would have been considered very bad five years ago. We'll just have to wait and see, I guess."

"How was the interview?" he asked.

"Is that what it was?" I asked. "It seemed more like an interrogation."

"He would have taken you into another room for that," he said.

"Then what was all that 'where were you' and 'how mad were you' stuff?"

"Just routine."

"That's what he said," I replied. "That's what you all say."

"Look, babe," he said, in a soothing tone, "you're not a suspect, okay? Not this time. It really is just routine to question the ex-spouse."

As I ate I was looking past Jakes at some of the people on the steps, and that was when I saw her. She had come out of the building, then walked quickly down the stairs. My first urge was to chase after her, but what would I say?

When she hit the street she practically ran away from the building.

"Look," I said.

"Where?"

"That woman holding the red umbrella."

He turned his head, looked, but I could see he wasn't spotting her.

"Who is it?" he asked.

"Patti."

"Who?"

"Patti, she does my make-up on the show."

He looked around again, then at me.

"She's gone," I said, "but she came out of your building."

"What was she doing in there?" he wondered.

"That's what I want you to find out," I said. I told him about her phone call, and what George had found on the caller I.D.

"Maybe she was here reporting a burglary, or a stolen car?"

"And you call yourself a detective?" I teased. "It's too much of a coincidence that two people from the same show needed to come down here and talk to the police today." And then it hit me. "Oh my God! Oh my God! That's too weird!"

"What's too weird?"

I took a few moments to process it before answering.

"You're not going to believe this. Okay. So, when I was working the other night, I noticed a stamp on Patti's wrist. You know, like the ones you get at a club? It was a fleur-de-lis. Like ummm, that royal emblem thing? Right? You with me so far?"

"Yeah, I'm following. What about it?"

"Just now, at Rockland's desk, I happened to see a photo of Randy at the crime scene. That same emblem was tattooed on his arm!" I was very excited by the implications. Unfortunately, Jakes wasn't feeling it.

"Sooo, you're saying Patti had a stamp of a very common design and Randy had a tattoo of a similar design and you think, what?" He was giving me his skeptical detective tone and it bugged me.

"Jakes. Not similar. The same! It can't be a coincidence. I saw a napkin at Patti's make-up station, too. The napkin had that fleur-de-lis on it. It was for a club in Los Angeles. They have to be connected!"

"So you think she was here talking to Rockland about Randy?"

I gave him an "isn't it obvious" look.

"Did she know Randy?"

"I don't know," I said. "I guess it's possible they met, at a party or something." Jakes eyes were like little slits as he stared at me.

"What?" I asked.

"You're doing it again."

"Doing what again?" I asked innocently, although I knew damn well what he was saying.

"I told you you're not a suspect, didn't I? You remember that?"

"Yes."

"So then you don't have a reason to play detective, do you?"

"I'm curious," I said, "I didn't go out and look for this situation. It fell squarely in my lap! And you have to go back inside, anyway. Right?"

"I'll ask around," he said, leaning over to kiss me. "Should I take you and Sarah out to dinner tonight?"

"How can you be so blasé about this? I'm on to something. I don't know what, but it's something."

"See you tonight."

He got up and walked up the stairs. I stood up, prepared to walk down.

"I'm not getting involved. I'm just curious. Don't forget to ask around, Detective!" I called after him.

He waved a hand without looking back. I went down the stairs without looking back. I knew he was mildly annoyed with me but he'd still turn to watch me walk away.

He always did.

Chapter 10

I went home, thinking about what Jakes had said about me not needing to play detective.

A few times in the past few years I did have to play detective, once to clear myself, twice to find out who had killed one of my co-workers and an acquaintance. Was this so different? Maybe I wasn't a suspect, but Randy was my ex-husband. More importantly, he was my daughter's father. Wasn't that reason enough to find out who killed him? Besides, like I had told Jakes, I hadn't gone looking for this. It came looking for me. So it wasn't really my doing, right?

It was still early afternoon. More clouds were moving in off the horizon, which meant more rain on the way. I made myself some tea and contemplated the significance of the fleur-de-lis on Patti's wrist and Randy's arm. I thought about the napkin I had seen at Patti's make-up station. What had it said? *Trois* something? I had taken a little French in high school so I knew *"trois"* was French for "three". I decided to google it.

I grabbed my laptop and my tea and carried them outside so I could enjoy some sun before the next deluge. I opened up my computer and typed in "Trois nightclub in Los Angeles". Nothing came up. I pondered how Patti and Randy could know each other, if, in fact, they did. I sat there for a moment and watched the water. It made me want to throw on my wetsuit and go surfing. Unfortunately, with all the rain the waters at most Los Angeles beaches were too dirty so I hadn't been out in a long time. Sad to say, the run off from sewers made it dangerous for surfers. Ear infections, stomach ailments, not necessarily a risk you want to take just to catch a wave. It made me feel a little melancholy as I remembered that Randy and I had gotten interested in surfing together. One of those things we had done in Waikiki on our first vacation as a couple. We had a lot of fun together in those days. He was so handsome and charismatic and he was good to me. I know he loved me. He just loved money more. My money in particular.

I couldn't figure out how he would know Patti. I hadn't worked with her before "The Bare and the Brazen," and I started there long after Randy and I were finished. I guess they could have run into each other over the years at industry parties I had taken him to. Wouldn't Patti have mentioned that? Unless they were sleeping together and Patti was embarrassed to tell me.

Hmmmm.

Patti Dennis had been doing make-up on *The Bare and The Brazen* for thirty years. She had to be in her late fifties and she still had it going on. But Randy liked his women younger, and dumb. After me, I mean. I couldn't see Randy with Patti that way.

Or maybe Patti having the stamp and being at the police station was a coincidence, after all. I decided to stop thinking about it until I heard from Jakes.

Instead, I was back to thinking about how to tell Sarah that her daddy was dead. She understood about death as best she could for being seven. We'd had the talk when she had accidentally loved her hamster to death a couple of years ago. I decided I would explain that her daddy went to Heaven, and he would always watch over her and be her personal angel. She was smart, though, and inquisitive. She was going to ask me why he died. And how. And when she did ask, I would need to have an answer ready for her.

A big plop of water hit me squarely on the nose. I looked up and saw the clouds had moved back in and we were in for another soaker. I quickly gathered up my computer and hustled inside.

Chapter 11

I picked Sarah up from school and listened to her talk about her day as we drove home. She wanted me to know that she was the fastest girl in the second grade. She had come in third at recess, beat out by two boys, Jesse and Riley.

"Mom, I was all wet after, I ran so fast. Nobody could believe it!" she exclaimed. "I just kept trying and trying, but Jesse and Riley are just SO fast."

"That's amazing, Sweetheart! I'm so proud of you for trying hard."

I decided not to tell her about Randy until I heard what Jakes had to say. I knew I was hanging onto a slim hope, but maybe they'd solved the mystery of his death before dinner and at least I'd know more information when I told her.

Yeah, right.

When we got home she ran to her room to play with her "American Girl" dolls and I went to the kitchen to prepare dinner. I'd stopped at our corner grocery store and gotten chicken breasts, bread crumbs, shredded mozzarella and a bottle of red wine. I was going to make my old standby "Chicken Mozzarella". Quick, easy and something I knew Sarah and Jakes always liked.

I pounded the poor chicken breasts with a wooden mallet into very thin fillets. If they weren't dead before they certainly were now. Then soaked them in beaten eggs. I was coating them in the breadcrumbs and dropping them in sizzling olive oil when Jakes walked in the front door. As had become normal, Sarah ran to him and he picked her up. "You're getting so big! I can hardly lift you up anymore, Sarah," Jakes said.

"Daddy says the same thing. He says I must be eating bricks. Daddy's so funny, isn't he, Mom?"

I looked at Jakes, kind of stunned, then took a second to regain my composure and said, "Yes, he is, honey. But no bricks for you tonight. I made your favorite chicken dish. Wash your hands. It's time to eat."

Sarah ran off to the bathroom and Jakes faced me. "You haven't told her yet?"

"No." I said as I turned the fillets.

"Why not?"

I placed the breasts in a baking dish, sprinkled a generous amount of shredded Mozzarella on them and stuck them under the broiler to melt. I poured two glasses of Merlot and handed one to Jakes.

"First, I don't know how," I said. "Second, I was hoping you'd come over today with good news."

"Sorry to disappoint," he said. "Let's eat and then I'll tell you after Sarah's in bed."

We had dinner, thankfully, Sarah didn't mention her dad again. After several rousing games of "Connect Four" I put Sarah to bed. Jakes read her a story. It had become an evening ritual when he was over. After she had fallen asleep we sat side-by-side on the sofa and I poured us each another glass of wine.

"Somebody hit Randy on the back of the head before he went down the hill in that mud slide." Jakes said.

"Really? Are they sure he didn't fall and hit his head on something. I mean, how do they know he was hit on purpose?"

"They found some metal bits in the wound, made by something like a wrench. Definitely not an accident. He was hit with the cliché 'blunt instrument'".

"So it's definitely a murder investigation."

"Yes."

"And your friend, Rockland? He's in charge?"

"Not my friend," Jakes said. "He's new to the squad, but he's a fast tracker. On his way up. And yeah, he's in charge." He gave me a look. "And he's kind of an asshole."

"Jakes," I said, "I know what you're thinking. I am not getting involved." He was still giving me that look. "I mean it. I'm going to let the professionals handle this."

He still looked skeptical.

"Okay, so maybe I'll just get a little involved." I added.

"How little?" He sighed.

"Well, I already am involved, because of Patti. I swear she has a connection with Randy. I can feel it."

"You can 'feel it', huh?" He put his arm around me. "What am I going to do with you? I know there's nothing I can say to convince you to really let the professionals handle it."

I turned to him and kissed him. I looked into his dreamy brown eyes. "I haven't done so badly before, have I?"

"Besides almost ending up dead a few times? I guess not."

"Seriously." I kissed him again. "I'm just going to get a little involved."

"You know that officially, I can't work the case. It's Rockland's case."

"What if he asked you for help?"

"He won't ask. He knows my connection to you and besides, he already has a partner. There's no way he's going to ask me for help. We just don't like each other."

"What about Patti?" I asked. "What was she doing at Police Headquarters?"

"Rockland wasn't talking."

"Not the friendly, sharing type, huh?"

"Not when he figures he'll be my boss within a year or two."

"So we don't know if she was there to talk to him?"

"No," he said, "but she was there. I talked to some people who saw her."

"Where?"

"In the building."

"In an interrogation room?"

"Maybe."

"That's not very helpful."

"I know it."

We finished our wine, put the glasses down on the table. I sat back.

"I'll have to talk to her," I said.

"She's does your make-up, right?"

"Right."

"You could just start a conversation," he said reluctantly. "Talk about her phone conversation, or tell her you saw her at the Police Administration Building today."

"I was thinking the same thing."

"Still don't remember if she knew Randy?"

"She never met him through me. That much I know."

"Alex, do you know anybody who'd want to kill Randy?" he asked.

"Besides me? No."

"What about the other people he swindled?"

"They all got their money back from their insurance company, remember?" I asked. "He was careful about who he robbed."

"Except for you."

"Yeah."

"Okay, so they got their money back," he said. "But maybe one of them was still mad enough to do it. Do you know any of them?" he asked.

"I met some of them, over the years." I answered. "It might be interesting to track them down and ask a few questions. You know, just for curiosity's sake."

"Does that still get categorized as a 'little involved?'" he asked.

I hesitated. "Probably not."

"Then I guess I'll have to get a little involved, too," he said, "Look, I'm kind of curious how Randy died. I have a vested interest."

"Am I your vested interest?" I snuggled into him.

"Yes. But so is Sarah. I want to make sure you're both safe and that this in no way has a connection to you."

I sat up.

"Oh my God! You're right! I hadn't thought about that. What if someone has it out for me, too?"

"Hold on. Don't panic," he said, soothingly. "That's a very slim chance. I just want to make sure my girls are safe."

"Your girls?" I got all teary eyed. "I really like the sound of that." I kissed him again, a little longer this time. Chivalry was not dead.

"Let's come up with a plan of attack. Nothing full on. It's us just getting 'a little involved.'"

"We can do that," I said, putting my arms around him. "In bed."

Chapter 12

We went to bed and made love, and then while I lay in the cradle of his arms, we hatched a plan. He told me how he would handle Randy's old customers.

"How will you know if they're lying to you?"

"You have to watch while you talk," he explained.

"Watch what?"

"Their faces," he said. "Body language. People do certain things when they lie. They look away. They clasp their hands tightly together. Compress their lips. Bite their lip. Little things, Alex. If you watch carefully, you see it."

"Is that more important than what they actually say?" I asked.

"Sometimes it is."

"I can do that. I've got a good bullshit meter. I'm an actress. I bullshit for a living."

"You just have to be sure that while you're watching them for lies, you make sure you tell the truth."

"Okay."

"You have to work tomorrow?"

"Yes, most of the morning, part of the afternoon."

"So tomorrow you'll talk to Patti."

"I haven't known her all that long. But I think I'll know if she's lying."

"Watch her carefully."

"Anything else?" I asked.

"Yes." He squeezed me tightly. "Time to go to sleep."

I felt him against my butt.

"Are you sure?" I asked.

"I'm sure," he said. "You need your rest. You'll need to be alert."

"Okay."

I snuggled back against him.

"You're bad," he said in my ear.

I wiggled back against him and said, "I just want to be sure you're alert."

We made love again in the morning, and then I made breakfast for all of us.

"I'll take Sarah to school if you want," Jakes said, at the table.

"Yaaay!" Sarah said, clapping her hands.

"No, that's okay," I said, "I want to do it."

"Awww, Mom!"

"Finish your cereal," I said to her.

"Jakes has a nicer car than we do."

I looked at him and he raised his eyebrows helplessly.

"No, he doesn't. What about Marilyn?" I asked. Marilyn is my Porsche Speedster. Classic.

"You won't let me ride in Marilyn except on special occasions. You said it's not safe."

"It's not. But my explorer is pretty nice. Isn't it?"

"The surfboard racks are always loose and they make that funny sound when you drive." She put a spoonful of Cheerios in her mouth.

"All right," I said, "Jakes can take you to school."

"Yaaaay!"

"Get your books."

As she ran to her room he came up behind me while I stood at the sink and encircled my waist with his arms.

"What made you change your mind?" he asked in my ear. I got the chills, as I always did when he spoke—or breathed—into my ear.

"I decided I want to make a few calls this morning before I go in."

"Are we still gonna play detective?" he asked.

"Yes, we are."

He kissed my neck and stepped away. "But you're only gonna talk to Patti. Leave the rest to me."

"All right."

"Sarah!" he yelled.

"Comiiiiing!"

She came into the kitchen to kiss me goodbye, put her arms around my neck. I got a whole different set of chills.

"See you later, Sweetie," I said. "I'll pick you up, later."

"Okay."

"I'll try to get the surfboard racks tightened."

She smiled and said, "Okay, Mommy."

"I love you."

"I love you, too."

"Sarah?"

"Coming, Jakes!" she yelled.

She picked up her back pack and ran to the door.

"I'll talk to you later," he said, blowing me a kiss from the door. It was one of the reasons I loved him. He was never afraid to blow me a kiss. Men just didn't do that, anymore.

I watched from the window as they drove away, then dialed my mother.

After telling my mother about Randy and assuming her she didn't need to come home, I hung up and dialed George's number.

"I was just getting ready to go in."

"I'm going to question Patti today."

"What happened yesterday?"

"I saw her at police head—I mean, the Police Administration Building. I saw her coming out, but that's all I know."

"So she didn't see you?"

"No."

"Who did she talk to?"

"I don't know."

"Jakes can't tell you? Or won't?"

"Can't. He's not the investigating detective on this case."

"No, of course not," George said. "You're involved. There's a conflict of interest. So what are you gonna do?"

"We're going to find out who killed Randy," I said. "I'm doing it for Sarah. Jakes is doing it for Sarah and me."

"Won't he get in trouble?"

"Only if he gets caught."

"And you're gonna start with Patti?"

"I just want to find out if she went to talk to the police about Randy's murder," I said. "Or if she went for some other reason. Then I—we—can eliminate her from a list of suspects."

"Wow," he said.

"What?"

"You talk like him," George said. "You talk like a cop."

"Yeah, well, comes from spending so much time with one."

"My mom ended up talking like a plumber," he said.

I frowned. "Your father wasn't a plumber."

"I know," he said. "Do you think that means my mother was having an affair with one?"

"I'll see you at the studio, George."

Chapter 13

"Stop! Your eyes are all over the place," Patti said. My eyes moved from side to side when I had a lot on my mind. Not good when someone has a pointy brush near your cornea.

Patti was usually very patient with us actors. Having to do beauty make-ups and special effects make-ups (cuts, bruises, etc.) while we ran lines (rehearsed), chatted with one another, moved around and got ourselves coffee. I have to admit we could be very annoying sometimes.

This morning was different. Patti seemed preoccupied and a little on edge. Usually we would talk while she made me up. Just superficial stuff. I don't think I ever had a conversation with her that didn't take place with me sitting in her chair. Not a deep one, anyway. She was kind of a quiet person. Except when she had a few drinks. I remember seeing her at one of our Christmas parties. Give her some tequila and she'd be dancing on a table top by night's end.

But she hadn't had any drinks this morning and she wasn't responding to my small talk. And she didn't gossip. So I was going to have to be direct.

"Alex, you have to sit still!" she snapped.

"I saw you, yesterday," I blurted. So much for Jake's coaching.

"Oh? Where?"

"On the balcony," I said. "You were on the phone in the rain. It looked like you were upset."

She stood up straight and stared at me, blinking.

"I . . . got the bad news, that two more soaps had been cancelled," she said. "I was so emotional I had to leave."

"Please. You had to leave because the shows got cancelled?"

"Like I said, I was too emotional and I needed a break." She was using a black eyeliner pencil under my eye. And in it.

"Ow!"

"See? We shouldn't be talking while I'm trying to do you! Now stop. I'll be done in a sec." She bent to finish my make-up, but I wasn't done. I jerked my head back and she stood up straight again.

"Something else?" she asked.

I considered being a little more cagey then decided screw it. I figured I'd just put it out there. "Yes," I said. "I saw you again later in the day."

Now she got a wary look on her face. "Oh? Where?"

"At the Police station."

She stood very still, her brain working.

"Why were you talking to the police, Patti?"

She didn't answer. She was still trying to think of an explanation.

"Patti?"

"I, uh . . ."

"It wasn't the cancellations, was it?" I asked. "You were talking to the police on the phone."

She compressed her lips. Her eyes started to dart about. According to Jakes, she was about to lie.

"Patti . . . did you know Randy?" I asked. "Is that what this was about?"

She stared at me, and then a resigned look came over her face and she said, "Oh, God."

I hadn't been called to the set yet, so I took Patti to my dressing room so we'd be able to talk in private.

"Okay, Patti," I said. "Tell me about you and Randy."

"It's not what you think."

"What do I think? Did you have a relationship with him?"

"Yes, but . . . not what you think."

"I still don't know what it is you think I think."

"I did meet Randy while you were married, but only once or twice in passing at parties," she said. "I don't think you and I even knew each other, then. He didn't remember me when . . ."

"When what?"

"When we met again, a few weeks ago."

"Where?"

"At a club."

"What club?"

"A club," she said.

"In L.A.?"

She nodded.

"I had no idea you were such a club rat, Patti," I said. But it didn't surprise me that Randy was.

"I'm not a club rat," she said. "Not the kind of club you're talking about."

"Patti," I said, "you're not being very clear, here."

"I met Randy at a club a few weeks ago," she said. "I recognized him, he didn't recognize me until I told him who I was. We became . . . friends."

I hoped what I was thinking wasn't showing on my face. Like I said before, Randy liked his women young and dum—, after me, I mean. But I guess there's always an exception. After all, it was all the rage to be a cougar, these days. Patti would certainly have qualified, having ten years or more on Randy.

"I know what you're thinking," she said.

Uh-oh, I still wasn't sure what I was thinking. But I didn't want her to know that.

"I don't blame you, Alex—"

"Patti—"

We both got interrupted by Herbie's voice calling for me to be on the set.

"I have to go," I said. "Can't you just tell me what you know?"

We stood up awkwardly.

"Not much. And I can't talk now—not here," she said and then resignedly, "but I can show you, later."

"Show me what?" I asked impatiently.

"Meet me tonight."

"Where are we going?" This was getting stupid.

"Clubbing," she said. "But not the kind of clubbing you're used to."

Actually, I wasn't used to much clubbing, at all. It wasn't something that was usually at the top of the priority list for single mothers. At least not this one.

"Are you talking about Trois ou Plus?" I played my trump card and definitely got what I was hoping for.

She stared at me and for a moment I thought her jaw was going to hit the floor.

"How did you know?" She could hardly speak the words.

"I saw a napkin with that name on it in your, uh, on the floor . . . you must have dropped it." I lied to her because I didn't want her to know I had been snooping.

She actually looked a little scared.

Herbie starting calling for me again, with a more adamant tone in his voice. That was never good.

"You better go before he has a stroke," she said as she reached into her purse. "I'll meet you in front of this address at ten p.m." She handed me the same napkin I'd seen.

"That late? I have to work tomorrow. Oh God, and I have a love scene, too."

"Believe me," she said, "where we're going, that's not late."

Where exactly was that? I looked at the napkin she had given me. It read: Trois ou Plus, 710 S. Alameda, Los Angeles.

She was walking out the door when she suddenly turned around. "Do you have a cowboy hat? And chaps, maybe?"

"What?"

"It's cowboy night at the club. Whatever you can dig up will be fine." Then she hurried out of my room.

I turned and looked at myself in the mirror. "Cowboy night?" I said. "Really?"

Chapter 14

I got home mid afternoon, called Tonja and asked if we could meet at her place and maybe have some coffee. I had an hour before I had to get Sarah and thought we could catch up, but I had an ulterior motive. I needed someone to watch Sarah while I went out "clubbing" with Patti.

"Would you mind if I came to your place?" she asked. "Mine's a mess!" I told her I didn't. It dawned on me after we'd hung up that I'd never actually been to her place since she moved in.

While waiting for Tonja to arrive, I pulled out the napkin I'd gotten from Patti. It looked like your basic bar napkin, I assumed Trois ou Plus to be a garden variety dance club, so why had Patti said it wasn't like any club I had ever been to?

Tonja was due any second so I went to the kitchen and made coffee then went to the cupboard and pulled out a couple of brownies I had gotten at the corner grocery store. The kind of brownies that are iced with butter cream frosting? That damned store had the best bakery. Okay, my name is Alexis Peterson, and I am a chocaholic. Not good when you have to simulate mad, passionate love the next day. After all, you wanted your body to look good when you were half naked on television. But I decided to throw caution to the wind and I took a bite.

"Hey, hey," she called out, coming through the front door I'd left unlocked.

"Coffee and brownies?" I asked, coming out of the kitchen with two cups and plates.

"Oh my God, I hate you! I can't eat the brownie. I swear I make it my life's work to still be able to get into my Laker's uniform. I would be just devastated if I couldn't fit my fanny into those yellow short shorts."

She looked at the brownies with so much desire in her eyes I started to feel like I should hide them. Before I could, her hand darted out and grabbed one, the biggest one. "Okay, just one bite." She tore into that thing like it was her last meal. I always say when you deprive yourself of something it turns you into a binger. Case in point.

"One won't hurt me," she said as she licked her fingers.

I have to admit I was a little taken aback. I couldn't help wondering if she was bulimic. I handed her a napkin to wipe the crumbs from her face when she grabbed my wrist to look at it.

"Wow," she said. "You surprise me, Alex."

"Good brownies, huh? I know. When I'm PMSing I go through . . ."

"That's not what I'm talking about. The napkin." A sly smile crept over her face. "I had no idea you were into . . . that," she said, waving the napkin in my face. Stupidly, I'd handed her my evidence. I took it back.

"Dance clubs? I've been to a few."

She stared at me, the sly smile growing into a wide grin.

"What?" I asked.

"Do you really think that's a dance club?"

"Well . . . I assumed. What other kind of club could it be?"

"So . . . you've never been there?"

"No," I said, "never."

She sipped her coffee and continued to look amused. It pissed me off.

"Okay, stop looking at me like that and tell me what's going on."

"That," she said, taking the napkin back and waving it around like a flag, "is a swingers club."

"Swingers?" I said. "You mean like keys in a bowl swingers? I thought that went out with the sixties."

"No," she said, "you're thinkin' of wife swapping. This is swingin'."

"So people go there to have sex? With somebody?"

"With somebody, anybody and everybody."

I frowned. So this was where Patti and Randy met? I needed to re-group, here. This had never crossed my mind. I didn't know which one surprised me more. Well, okay Patti. Randy, I at least knew, could be a little twisted and leaned toward the slightly dangerous things in life. But Patti? Always so professional and quiet a swinger? I mean she looked great even if she was pushing 60. And I knew she could get a groove on after some shots of tequila, but who knew her groove was that kind of groove? Yeah, that was the bigger surprise.

"Why do you have this napkin, I mean, if you've never been there?" Tonja asked, a little skeptical. "Research for a part?"

It occurred to me to seize that as an excuse, but then I thought no. If I was going to find out who killed Randy, I was really going to need someone to watch Sarah from time to time. So, I decided to be truthful.

I told her the whole story.

"Oh my God," she said, after I finished. "Alex!" She reached out and put her hand on my shoulder. "I'm so sorry."

"It's okay," I said. "I got over Randy a long time ago. It's Sarah I'm worried about."

"You haven't told her yet?"

"I want to be able to tell her how and why her daddy died," I said. "I mean, that he was murdered . . ."

"You're gonna tell her he was murdered?" she asked. "And why?"

I drank some coffee.

"Maybe it's for my own benefit. Maybe I need to know the how, the why and the who before I tell her. I don't know. I'm just trying to do what feels right, Tonja."

"Well, I can see that, I guess."

"I need your help, though," I said.

"Sure, I'll be glad to help. What do you want me to do?"

"I have to go to this club tonight to meet Patti," I said.

"The make-up artist who knew Randy?"

"Yes, I still have to find out how she knew Randy. Why he had the clubs logo tattooed on his arm? What does that mean? I'm hoping to get something out of her tonight."

"You think she knows who killed him?"

"Maybe not exactly," I said. "But if she and Randy were in that life, maybe she can point me to some people he pissed off. He was good at that."

"And you think he made somebody mad enough to kill him?"

"It's obvious that's what he did," I said. "I just need to find out who."

"So, you're goin' to this club tonight?"

"Yes, and I need you to watch Sarah."

Excitedly, she said, "I have a better idea. Let me go with you."

"Why?" I asked. "Have you been there before?"

"Not to that club, but I've been to others. There are certain . . . protocols you'll have to adhere to."

"Yeah, so I found out. Patti said that tonight was 'cowboy' night. I need chaps or . . . something cowboyish. Are there more things I need to know?"

"Definitely," she said with a smile.

"And you know them?"

"I had a boyfriend for a short time who was into it," she said. "I went with him a few times, but I could never . . . you know . . . I just . . . watched."

I studied her and asked, "You just . . . watched?" Her eyes were dart-ing around so I knew she was lying. Jakes was a master!

"I just watched," she said. "We broke up soon after that. Anyway, you'll need someone who knows the ropes, Alex."

"I'll be meeting Patti there."

"Yeah, but you don't know what she's up to, do you?"

"Patti? She's not a danger to me."

"Did you ever think of her as bein' a swinger? Or knowin' your ex?" She had a very valid point.

"Well, no . . ."

"I think you need somebody to watch your back. Do you want to tell your boyfriend where you're goin'?"

"No!" I said. "I don't want him to know quite yet. He'd probably try to stop me."

She smiled and asked, "He wouldn't, maybe, want to go with you?"

"Well, if you mean for pleasure, no," I said. "He'd never be into that." That made me think. Would he? He's not very good at sharing and actually, neither am I. "If you mean as a cop, then again, no. I think he'd make me stay home and go meet Patti himself. I'm not so sure I'd want him going there without me."

"Then you need me," she said, "to be your partner in crime. And . . . to help you get dressed."

Chapter 15

We talked a bit about who should watch Sarah. Tonja said she sometimes worked with a teenaged girl while programming computers, but I thought maybe I had a better idea. I said I'd let her know and she left with the promise of returning around 8:00 so we could get ready together. I told her I'd call her before then about the babysitter.

Then I called Georgie.

"I have a better idea," he said.

"What?"

"I'm going with you girls."

"Georgie—"

"Who's always been your best wing man, Sweetie?" he asked.

"You, but— this isn't your normal kind of club, George." I hesitated because I wasn't sure what I should say to him. Patti and George worked together and I was pretty sure she wouldn't want him knowing about her "secret" life. "Look, stay where you are. I'll get right back to you." I disconnected the call before he could say anything and then I called Patti.

"Make-up," she answered.

"Hi, Patti, it's Alex. I was hoping you'd still be there."

"What's up? Still coming tonight?" She didn't sound too thrilled to be hearing from me.

"Oh, yeah. Here's the thing. A girlfriend of mine saw the napkin you gave me and told me what kind of a club Trois ou Plus is." I waited for a response and just got silence. So I went on. "I don't want to make things uncomfortable for you but, uh, George wants to come."

"Oh my God! Did you tell him about the club, too?"

"No! I mean, not yet. I wanted to talk to you first."

I waited for her to say something but all I heard was her breathing on the other end. "I promise we won't say anything to anyone about this, and your, uh, 'lifestyle' if that's what you're worried about."

"Wait a sec." She must have put her hand over the mouthpiece because I heard muffled voices. "I'm taking the phone into the hall." She was whispering now. I heard her take a deep breath. "Fuck it. I'm screwed. Go ahead and bring him, but no one else."

"Well, I kind of have to bring my friend. She knows about the club and I could use the help. If you know what I mean."

She took a beat before answering. "Fine. I'll see you at ten."

She hung up on me. That was weird. But so was everything else about Patti, lately. I called George back.

"You have got to be kidding me! Patti? The most professional person on the planet, a swinger? I never would have guessed it!" I waited for him to get off the ceiling before answering.

"She said I could bring you, George, but I don't know. I don't want to make her feel more uncomfortable than she already does. We all work together and I'm sure she doesn't want this getting out. Talk about embarrassing. And it could cost her her job."

"I won't say a thing. You know me. I'll keep it zipped."

"I don't know, George."

"All the horrible secrets you've told me over the years. Have I ever betrayed you?" I wasn't exactly sure what "horrible" secrets he was talking about but I let it slide for the moment. "You don't know what's going to happen at that club, Alex," he said. "Besides, I've always wanted to go to a real swinger's club."

"Really? Okaaay, but it's not a gay swinger's club—"

"All the better. I'm going to disguise myself as a straight man. An adventurous, woman loving straight man. I love it! I have to go with you, Sweetie. When was the last time we had some fun? Huh?" he asked. "You really do need somebody with you that you can count on."

This covert operation was getting more crowded by the minute. Before I could protest again or ask about my "horrible" secrets he asked, "And who's gonna do your hair? You need to have swinger's hair! Something circa nineteen sixty-five. We need to rat it up really high. What should I wear? Maybe a jumpsuit? How dope would that be? What are you gonna wear? Something sexy. Like a dress straight out of Mad Men?"

"George! This isn't a role I'm playing. Swinger's don't dress any differently than anyone else." I paused. "Well, actually they do. Patti told me that tonight is cowboy night and I have to wear something western. Tonja's coming over at eight. We're going to get ready together."

"Cowboy night? That settles that. I am not taking no for an answer. I'm going. I have the best cowpoke outfit from two Halloweens ago. I have something for you, too!"

"No thanks, Georgie. I got it covered."

"Okay. But if you change your mind—" I assured him I wouldn't. "I'll be there at eight," he said. "I'll do both your hair. Wouldn't Tonja love that?"

"Well, yeah, what chick wouldn't," I said, "but we still need a babysitter for Sarah."

"No problem, I'll bring him with me."

"Wayne? Does he have the time?" Wayne was George's longtime partner and my second closest friend in the world.

"He's between projects," George said. "Plus he loves Sarah."

"And she loves him. Okay, I'll call Tonja and tell her what's up."

"Good," he said. "Then we'll be there at eight."

"And Georgie?"

"Yeah?"

"Let's not go too over the top with the costume, okay? I mean, don't dress as a cow or a horse, please."

I was thinking back to the Halloween party at Hef's a couple years ago. George had dressed as a big fluffy lamb.

"We don't want to attract too much attention," I told him.

"Sweetie," he said, "we don't wanna stand out for the wrong reason, either. If you know what I mean?" I think I heard him wink.

Chapter 16

"George, you are a car snob," I said.

"Why? Because I don't want to be in your beat up Explorer with those strappy things slapping all over the place?"

"They are surfboard racks, George. And who cares, anyway?" I was getting tired of the people I loved picking on my Explorer.

"I want to arrive in style, Sweetie. We have people to impress." This coming from the man who had on cow print chaps and a ten gallon hat.

Tonja had fared better. She was wearing a suede miniskirt and cowboy boots with a rhinestone bustier and a cute cowboy hat. I basically had on the same thing she did except my skirt was denim and I had added a kerchief. Thank God I never threw anything away. I had found these clothes in a storage box in my garage, leftovers from the 80's.

"Are you sure we're in the right area? This doesn't look like any club neighborhood to me. Where the hell is this place?" George asked.

"This is right," Tonja piped in. "These kinds of clubs are always out in the boonies. So as not to attract any attention. Keep driving! It should be on the left."

I wasn't too sure about that. On the left were abandoned warehouses and industrial parks.

"By the way, Alex, what did you tell Jakes about tonight?" Tonja asked.

"I told him the truth. That I was going out to a club with you and George."

"How'd he take it?" George asked.

"Fine."

"Fine?" he asked.

"Yeah, fine. He's working. He's fine," I said.

George turned in his seat towards me.

"You told him that you were going to a swinger's club?"

"Not exactly. I said I was going to a club."

George was quiet for a second. "He's gonna be pissed," he said simply. I shot him a look.

"Maybe we took a wrong turn," I said scanning the street. "Wait! There's Patti!"

She was dressed in very tight, white leather chaps with fringe all over.

Her boobies were spilling out of her matching white leather vest and she was holding a white cowboy hat in her hand. I guess she was trying to be discreet by wearing a black overcoat. It wasn't working.

"OMG! Look at Patti!" George couldn't contain himself. "She's all in leather and fringe. And look at her boobs!"

"Take it easy, George. You're supposed to act cool. We don't want to upset her." Jeez. I can't take him anywhere.

She pointed to a parking lot across the street as she ran across to meet us.

"Pull in, George. Where that guy is," I said as we drove up to a gated parking lot.

There looked to be about 50 or so cars there already. Patti was speaking to the security guard in front of the gate. I saw her gesture towards our car and he nodded. He unlocked the gate and pulled it open. As we drove through I looked at Patti. She seemed nervous and kind of excited, too. She also had on a lot of make-up. Not the Patti I knew from work, at all.

We pulled into a space the guard had indicated. I got out of the car and put on my coat. It was cold but I looked at the night sky and saw that it was clear.

"We don't need our umbrellas guys. It looks like a nice night for a change." Tonja looked up and then threw her umbrella back in the car. We all walked over to Patti.

"Did you guys bring your I.D.s? You'll need them to get in." She looked at George with a mix of embarrassment and resignation. She also looked kind of pissed. "Hi, George," she said.

"Hey, Patti! You look so different. But good different. Really good. Wow. I never knew your boobs could do that." I elbowed George in his ribs. He winced but thankfully shut up.

"Hi Patti. I'm Tonja. I've been to a few of these clubs before. Well . . . I never did anything, though. I had a boyfriend who was into this lifestyle and so I went a couple of times. Followed him around. But just out of curiosity." She wouldn't stop. "I used to be a Laker's Cheerleader, in the nineties? The championship years? You wouldn't believe the stuff players and even some of the cheerleaders were into. It was never really my thing, though. I'm a small town girl at heart, ya know . . . ?"

Patti wasn't buying it.

"Right. Follow me," she said curtly as she led us across the street. Which, by the way, was completely deserted.

As we approached the building I saw that it was indeed a warehouse. And it was huge. It had all sorts of graffiti painted on its walls; trash was strewn everywhere. It looked like some homeless people had set up camp; there were large boxes and a shopping cart filled with old clothes out front. I was feeling a little anxious about going into this place. I wasn't sure what I expected but this was definitely *not* it. Patti stopped in front of a nondescript metal door.

"Before we go in, there are a few things I need to tell you." She looked at each of us closely. "I called the owner and said I was bringing some friends tonight that I would vouch for. So please, don't do anything stupid. Such as do not, I repeat, *do not* take pictures with your phones. And," she said, looking at George, "try not to look like what you're seeing is shocking. George, you already look stunned and you haven't seen anything, yet. Dial it down, okay? I don't want to make anyone feel uncomfortable here. These people come here to have fun and they need to feel safe." I looked at George and he seemed insulted. "Also, don't use your first names. Alex, we'll call you April tonight. George, you can be John."

"I don't want to be John, Patti. I want to be hmmm . . . Fabrizio!"

Patti rolled her eyes. "Fine. You're Fabrizio. Tonja is Tina. Okay? And just in case, if you happen to see someone you know, please don't run up to them and make a scene. Discretion is everything."

What she said made perfect sense. I pulled my coat around me and glanced at Tina and (God) Fabrizio. "Ready? Let's go!" Then I reached for the door's handle.

Patti stopped me. "Not so fast. There's something else you need to know. Chick's rule here."

Okay, I thought to myself. "What does that mean, exactly?" I asked.

"Women call the shots at these clubs. What they say goes. So you ladies can go where you want but George here has to be with a woman at all times. No single men allowed wandering around. And no touching without permission."

"Are you kidding? Patti, we're here to observe not participate." Then I looked at Tonja. "Right, Tonja?"

"Yes, of course!" she said with wide, innocent eyes. "I told you this isn't my thing."

"Anyway," Patti continued, "I'll walk you through and show you around. Just do as I say. Did you bring cash? I don't think you'll want this to come up on your credit card."

"I've got it, I said as I went for my purse. "This is on me."

"Thanks, Alex," George said.

"Yeah, thank you! These places can be a little pricey, right Patti?" Tonja asked.

Patti looked at her and answered in a matter of fact way. "I guess that depends on how much you think having every fantasy you've ever had . . . fulfilled . . . is worth."

We all looked at each other as she opened the door and gestured with her hand. "Shall we?" she asked.

I took a deep breath and walked in.

Chapter 17

"Hello! Welcome!" a warm, silky voice said.

The walls of the small anteroom were draped in dark blue velvet curtains. The whole place was very dark. As my eyes adjusted I could see an attractive woman in her thirties sitting behind a mahogany desk. A large fleur-de-lis, like the one Randy had tattooed on his arm, was carved into the front of it. A small dragonfly Tiffany lamp sat on the desk barely illuminating her pale face. She had dark hair pulled back into a ponytail and was wearing a black cowboy hat. She got up and walked across a tapestry rug to the front of the desk to greet us. She was wearing a tight, halter style, black leather jumpsuit. Her breasts looked like they were ready to spill out.

"I knew I should have worn a jumpsuit!" George whispered to me.

"Hi, Natalie. These are the friends I told you about," Patti said.

Natalie held out a pale, almost translucent, hand to each of us. Her fingers were thin and tapered and her nails were long and painted in a bright red color. She wasn't just attractive, she was stunning.

"Hello, again, and welcome to Trois ou Plus. I assume Vivica told you about our rules?" She looked to each of us and we looked at each other. Who the hell was Vivica? Patti interjected, "Yes. I told them everything they need to know. They'll be fine."

"Good. That will be three hundred dollars. Cash please," Natalie said holding out her hand.

Wow. $300.00. "Is that three hundred apiece or what?" I asked her.

"Total. We generally charge one hundred and fifty per 'couple'. And since there are four of you . . ."

I reached into my purse and pulled out three one-hundred-dollar bills and handed them to her. As I did, she held my hand just a little too long. Oh right! Girls rule.

"Thank you," she said to me, smiling with her dark exotic eyes. "There's a bar down the hall and to the left, past all the theme rooms."

George and I nudged each other. "Theme" rooms? "There's also a dance floor in there. The DJ will be starting in about . . ." she looked at her diamond studded Rolex, ". . . about twenty minutes or so."

DJ? Honestly, a DJ? I thought to myself.

She reached for a crystal bowl that sat on her desk.

"Just in case?" She passed the bowl to each of us.

"How nice. Breath mints," George said reaching into the bowl.

Patti swatted his hands. "They're not breath mints, Fabrizio."

"Well, what are they . . . Vivica?"

"They're condoms. Safe sex or no sex."

"Of course! Always safe sex," I said as I grabbed a few. I threw a couple to George and Tonja.

"Wrists, please," Natalie said as she opened a drawer and pulled out a stamp. We all dutifully held out our arms as she stamped the fleur-de-lis on the inside of each of our wrists. Whatever they were using made the ink very dark and precise, like a tattoo.

Patti walked over to another door and opened it. A heavy curtain hung from the ceiling. As she pulled it aside Natalie said, "It's still early. There aren't too many people here, yet. Give it another hour. Oh, and have fun." She had a small smile on her face as she turned back to sit down.

We walked through the curtain and the door closed behind us. I suddenly felt like I was stepping into another world as I walked into the long dark hallway. It was empty and the walls were painted black and had small dimly lit sconces on either side. I could make out maybe four or five closed doors on the left with signs on them. On the right maybe two more doors. Each door had a small window next to it.

George reached for my hand. "What have you gotten me into, you crazy woman?" he whispered.

"Are you kidding me? You begged to come along. Don't blame me if this freaks you out."

"Just kidding. This'll be fun." He looked at me, worried. "Won't it?" I wasn't so sure what I'd call it. Patti turned around. "You coming?" she asked me.

"Yeah, of course. But what is this all about? What does this have to do with Randy's murder?"

"Shhhhh." Patti grabbed my hand pulled me into a corner. "I told you, just like I told the cops," she insisted, "I don't know anything about Randy's death."

Just then three couples exited a room down the hallway. They were laughing. Patti abruptly stopped talking and put on a smile. It looked more like a grimace, actually. The couples disappeared through another door further down the hall.

Patti glanced around nervously making sure no one was near us. "I just thought you should know a little more about your ex-husband. Maybe it'll lead somewhere. Now, I'll show you around and that's that. You're the amateur detective. You figure it out." She looked around again. "C'mon. I'm in a hurry."

Chapter 18

"Let's go!" Patti whispered as she led the way. I wasn't exactly sure why we were being so sneaky, but I took Patti's lead.

George and I headed down the hallway with Tonja following behind. I stopped at the first door and saw a sign that said Director's Room. I moved to the window, took a peek and couldn't believe what I was seeing. There was a raised platform at the front of the room surrounded by maybe 10–15 mattresses. One guy was sitting in a director's chair and a handful of people were on the beds engaging in things I'd only seen on Animal Planet. I must have looked shocked because George took off his hat and used it to push me out of the way.

"I wanna see! Move over." He looked in the window and screamed hoarsely.

"Shut up George!" Patti hissed. "Remember what I said? Get it together." She pushed him out of the way.

"What the heck was that, anyway? Did you see that guy's . . ." George asked.

"Just what it says on the door, George. It's the Director's Room," Patti explained. "The guy on the dais is . . . observing. The couples down below like to be observed. If you don't like who's watching you, you leave."

Then the door opened and a couple came out adjusting their costumes. I looked away, kind of embarrassed. They didn't seem to mind at all.

"Hi, y'all!" the woman said. She did a double take and then said, "Oh hiiiii." And smiled at me.

"Hi, there." I answered.

She was an attractive woman in her forties and looked kind of familiar but I couldn't place her.

Her date pulled her away, saying, "Let's get a drink and go to the Doctor's office."

"Again?" she replied. "I've had enough of that. I wanna go to jail." She pulled him close to her body. "You've been a very bad boy and I think you need to be locked up."

She put her arm around him tightly as they walked away.

"Okay, I guess it's jail for me!" he agreed.

She turned back and looked at me again and gave a little wave. Okay, that was kind of gross.

They disappeared into a room further down the hall. George looked like he was about to implode. "Do you know who that was?" He was swinging his hat around wildly. "That was Carla Miller. The channel five newscaster!"

"Aww. So that's where I'd seen her before", I said. She had recognized me and must have thought I was partying, too. Oops.

"Let's keep moving," Patti said, giving George a dirty look. She headed down the hall. I looked behind me and saw that Tonja was still glued to the window.

"Tina, you coming?"

She looked at me and blinked. "Oh, yeah. I'll catch up with you guys. I have to go to the ladies room." And she headed off in the other direction. Before I could ask her how she'd find us, she had turned the corner.

George and I looked at each other. "Do you think she'll be all right?" George asked me.

"I have a feeling she'll be just fine."

Patti stopped in front of another window. I looked in. This must be the 'Doctor's Office' because there was an exam table and a few people gathered around it dressed in Doctor's scrubs and masks. It looked like someone was on the table.

"This is so hedonistic," George said. "Mind blowing and fascinating, really. What it says about our society, I mean? The Romans engaged in this sort of thing and look what happened to their civilization."

I nodded and added, "So true, but I'm not one to judge. Who's to say what consenting adults should or shouldn't do. What I find so fascinating is how they can share their husbands and wives or significant others with other people without any fighting? If I ever saw Jakes with someone else, I'd have to kill him." Patti looked at me. "What? It's just a figure of speech, Patti. Really."

She looked a little skeptical. "Do we really need to have a dissertation on the social implications of this lifestyle choice right here? Right now?" she asked. "And it's Vivica!" Then she turned and continued down the hall. She was pissed. Was it because I had bullied her into taking us here? Maybe because her secret was out? Or was it something else?

We stopped at another door that said: Girls Only. I looked in the window not knowing exactly what to expect but it was empty.

"It's early," Patti explained. "It'll be full within the hour, I'm sure. It's a very popular room." She moved on down to the next window.

"I can't see anything," George said, squinting.

"That's because the window is painted black. This is the Scary Room. George and I both looked confused, and probably a little scared.

"What does that mean?" I asked.

"It's pitch black. So no one can see *anything*. Or any one for that matter. Nobody ever admits to going in there. But, well . . . it's *always* full. If you know what I mean."

"I know what you mean. And this is all very shocking in an interesting and perverse way. But what does it mean?" I asked. "If you're trying to tell me that Randy had some kinky sex habits, okay, I get it. Obviously, he had changed, because believe me he wasn't into this stuff when we were together." I was getting exasperated. "Why did you want me to see this? What does Randy's death have to do with all of it?"

"I told you before. I don't know anything about Randy's death, Alex." Patti hesitated before she added, "I just thought you should know." She seemed frustrated and resigned. "Follow me."

She furtively looked around and then led us to a dark corner. A door marked: Office with no window next to it was there. "I'm going to get a drink. I'll be right back."

"Wait a sec. You can't just leave us! Is this another theme room? Someone's playing secretary in there or something?"

She looked around again nervously. "Look, I've told you everything I know. I gotta go."

"Wait, Patti! What do I do now? What about . . ." But she was gone.

George and I looked at each other.

"Now what?" He asked me.

We were alone. No Tonya. No Patti. "I guess we go in."

Chapter 19

I turned the knob and slowly opened the door, not sure what we'd find in there. I half expected to see couples playing CEO and secretary games. But I was happy to see it was just an office. I let out a sigh of relief.

"What's in there?" George whispered behind me.

"Nothing that I can see. Just a desk, sofa, bookcase. It's an office." We both stepped inside and closed the door behind us. "For some reason Patti wanted me to come in here." I gave the place a quick once over but couldn't see anything. It was too dark. "I'd better nose around a little. Wait outside, George, and be my lookout. Knock twice if anyone comes by."

"I don't want to wait outside. What if someone wants to do something with me in one of those rooms?"

"Deal with it." I grabbed his hat and put it back on his head, then shoved him out the door.

I stepped further into the room and found a desk lamp. I turned it on and the room was bathed in a dim light. There was a long table behind the desk with papers on it. I was rifling through them when I heard two quick knocks. I ran to the door and slowly opened it. George was standing there. Alone.

"What?"

"Nothing. I just wanted to make sure you'd come out if I knocked." I gave him a look and closed the door again.

I went back to the papers but couldn't find anything of interest. It looked like cost sheets and other business related stuff. Nothing I recognized. I opened a few cupboards and pulled out some clothing.

"Ewww." I dropped them when I realized what they were. A policeman's uniform—probably used for the Jail room. Lovely.

I went to the desk and started opening up drawers. There was nothing of interest in the first three, except one had several packs of cigarettes. There was one more drawer at the bottom I hadn't gone through. I opened it and found files. Four were bound together. Each cover page had a large fleur-de-lis printed on it but a different name directly beneath. I quickly looked over the name: Cliff Dweller, Bobby McBalls, a few others. Were these people kidding? I put the files away and heard two quick knocks, again. This time they were more urgent. I peeked out the door. George came bursting in.

"You're not going to believe who I just saw going into the Doctor's Office!"

"Who?"

"My dentist! How crazy is that?"

"Your dentist? What? Did he see you?"

"No. I don't think so. I pulled my hat down. He was with his wife! Oh my God. I can never have him put a drill in me again! Have you found anything, yet? I'm getting nervous."

"Give me five minutes. Any sign of Tonja?"

"No. I think that girl is off exploring. Hurry!"

I pushed him back into the hall and closed the door, leaning on it. Then I looked around wondering what the hell Patti thought I would find so interesting in here. I saw a bookcase on the other wall and walked over to it. The books were varied, some on sports, some on travel. There were bookends and knick knacks interspersed along the shelves.

Then I saw it. A clay figure. It looked like it was supposed to be a dog or an animal of some sort. You could tell it had been made by a small child. And not just any child. It was made by Sarah. She had made it for her father when she was not quite three years old.

I felt like I'd been hit by a truck. To find something so personal in such a strange and random place was more than a little disturbing. I couldn't make any sense of it. What was this piece of my daughter's childhood doing on this bookshelf in this office in this kind of a club? It could only mean one thing. This was Randy's office.

I became frantic as I looked around the room again. What hadn't I seen before that I would see now?

I examined at the books more closely. Sure enough the travel books were all Randy. All about various cities and countries in South America. That was where Randy had run off to after he had stolen my money. I knew he had fallen in love with that part of the world and the number of books on the region confirmed it. Also, I realized now that the packs of cigarettes in the desk were his brand.

I scanned the walls and floor. Could something be hidden in them? Then my eyes fell back on the desk. I had been in the middle of looking through files when George interrupted me. I hurried back to the drawers, pulling files out, laying them on the desk under the lamp. *Knock-knock.*

"Shit! George! Not now!" I muttered under my breath. I kept going through the papers and saw one with Randy's signature on it. It was some kind of a purchase agreement. George poked his head in.

"We gotta go! Now!"

"Why? I'm just now on to something."

"Trust me. We gotta go!"

"Shit, shit, shit!" I quickly put the files away, ran back over to the bookcase and picked up the little clay dog Sarah had made. Should I take it? Would anyone miss it?

There were two very frantic knocks on the door again. I put the figurine in my purse and hurried out the door. And right into Natalie.

Chapter 20

"What are you doing in here?" she asked, looking alarmed. I glanced at George and his eyes were as big as saucers.

"Uh, I thought it was another theme room. You know, Secretary and boss shenanigans?" I said thinking on my feet. Natalie eyed me suspiciously as she opened the door and stepped into the office. She looked around and came back into the hall.

"You're not supposed to be in there. It's private."

"I'm so sorry." I put on my most innocent face. "I'm new to all of this. Sorry."

"I think you all need to leave." She wasn't being so warm and silky anymore. She was being downright mean. "Where's your friend?"

"You mean, Patti? I mean, Vivica?"

"No. The other one. Patti left."

"Patti left?" I asked.

Natalie nodded.

"Fifteen minutes ago."

That was news to me. Why would Patti leave without telling us?

"And *he's* not supposed to be wandering around alone, remember?" she said gesturing to George.

"Oh, yeah. The 'Girl's Rule' rule." George said. "But I wasn't really wandering. I was just kind of loitering."

She took out a key from her pocket and locked the office door.

"Find your friend and leave. You've got five minutes." And she left.

"I wonder what the bouncer looks like, here?" George said.

"This is so bizarre." I had sweat on my upper lip. "We gotta go." We started down the hall; I was holding onto George for dear life.

"Did you find anything?" George whispered. He pried my fingers off his wrist.

"You're not going to believe it."

"Tell me." We turned the corner and there was Tonja, standing square-ly in front of the Jail Room window. She was looking around wildly, like she was lost, and when she saw us this look of relief came over her face.

"Oh, hi, you guys! I was looking for you!" She seemed tipsy and I saw that her skirt was on, well, backwards. George saw it, too.

"We're leaving." I said, leading them both to the exit.

"Oh, so soon?" She was very disappointed.

"Natalie wants us to leave," George interjected.

"Oh Natalie, schmatalie! I don't want to leave. Uh, I think I'll stay awhile. I ran into some people I know." She got very close to my face and I could smell whiskey. "I wish they had a Basketball Room. I'd rock it! Go Lakers!" I backed away and was losing my patience, fast. "Natalie really wants us to go. Now."

"I'll have my friends vouch for me."

"And how will you get home, Tonja?" George asked. He wasn't so patient either.

"I'll get a ride with one of my pals." She seemed very fidgety, anxious to get back to . . . what? "I'm just going to stay and have another cocktail. And dance." She lowered her voice. "You know."

"Riiight. Dance. Okay." I asked.

"That would be great! I'll see you tomorrow!" Off she went in the direction of the Jail. I heard a distant "Go Lakers!" coming from some-where.

George and I looked at each other.

"So much for this not being her 'thing'," he said.

"Never mind. Let's just go."

"What did you find?"

"I'll tell you in the car."

George and I were on the 10 Freeway, heading toward Venice Beach. A light rain had begun to fall.

"George, I think we should go to Patti's. Where does she live?"

"Why should we go there? Now?"

"Because I want to know why she just left us there?" I said.

"Get off on Highland and take it towards the Hollywood Hills."

"I've got to call Wayne and tell him we'll be later. Home!" I shouted out. The phone rang twice and Wayne picked up. "Hi Wayne. How are you and Sarah?"

"We're good. She's sound asleep. How are you two?"

"Fine. I just wanted to let you know we'll be a little later than we thought. We're stopping by Patti's on the way home."

"Is everything all right?" Wayne knew enough about our antics to be concerned.

"We're fine, Sweetie," George yelled out. "You're not going to believe the stories we have to tell!"

"I can't wait to hear all about it. Be safe out there, you two!"

"We will!" George and I yelled out at the same time, then looked at each other as I disconnected the call.

"What did you find in that office? C'mon. Enough with the suspense."

I reached into my purse and pulled out the clay figure. I carefully placed it in his hand. "I found this. Can you believe it?"

George looked from his hand to my face a couple of times.

"What the hell is it?" he asked.

"Sarah made it for Randy when she was about three years old," I explained. "And I found it in that office on the bookshelf."

"What does it mean?"

"What do you mean what does it mean? It means that had to be Randy's office. Why else would it be on that bookcase? And I found his brand of cigarettes in one of the drawers," I answered as I turned on the windshield wipers. "And *that* means Randy worked there, at the very least. Maybe it was his club. I don't know." I was very nervous and excited. George seemed less enthused. "Don't you think this is amazing? This is what Patti wanted me to see!"

"It looks like a clay lump. How do you know Sarah made it?"

"Clearly, it's a dog, George. And I know my daughter's artwork. Sarah gave it to him the last Father's Day he was here. Before he left us." I grabbed it out of his hand and put it back in my purse.

"If you say so, Sweetie." He didn't look very convinced.

"I do say so. I gotta call Jakes." I yelled out "Call Jakes!" and I heard his cell phone ringing. His voicemail picked up. "Jakes, I need to talk to you ASAP. Call me as soon as you can. Everything's okay. I just found something out, tonight. About Randy. Call me. Love you." I disconnected my cell.

"He's gonna be pissed," George finally said.

Boy, I thought is he ever!

Chapter 21

George directed me to Patti's house, in the hills off Mulholland Highway. I parked in front, sprang out of the car and ran to the door.

"Wait for me!" George shouted, moving more slowly. He ran to catch up, though, and when he reached me he was out of breath. "You don't know who or what's in there."

"Oh, shit," I said turning the knob.

"What?" he asked, coming up alongside me.

"It's not locked."

"So? That doesn't mean it's okay to go in."

"Whoops!" I said as I "accidentally" pushed on the door.

"Wait, wait!" he hissed, grabbing my arm. "Call Jakes!"

"I did call him, remember?" I asked, lowering my voice to match his. "He didn't answer."

"Yeah, but . . . we don't know who's in there," he said, again.

"What if Patti's in there and she's hurt? Maybe she needs help?"

"Then she should've stayed with us."

"Look, George, you can stay out here and wait," I said.

"Well, okay . . ."

"Maybe somebody will come running out and you can deal with them."

I pushed open the door and stepped in. Behind me he said, "Wha— who's gonna run out—hey, wait!"

He followed me into the house.

Patti wasn't there, hurt or otherwise. Everything looked fairly neat, except a few of her dresser drawers were open in the bedroom.

"There's nothing in them, George. Check her closet."

"What am I looking for?"

"See if she's taken her clothes out of there, too. Remember not to touch anything."

"Wha—? Oh." He got it. "Okay."

I walked around the room, making sure to take my own advice. I heard George open a closet, turned and snapped, "Helloooo! Don't touch anything! Fingerprints, remember?"

"Then how do I look—oh, okay."

He slid the closet door open the rest of the way, using his shirt tail.

"Not much left in the way of clothes."

"Maybe she split," I said, opening a drawer next to her bed. Thank goodness it was empty. I was kind of afraid what I might find there. "I bet she ran back here from the club, packed and left."

"Why would she do that?"

"Maybe she saw somebody in the club who scared her. You saw how she was. Definitely in a rush to get out of there. But when she left us by that office, she knew I'd go in. Maybe she thought I'd recognize something that would tell me it was Randy's."

"Alex, don't you think that's giving Patti way too much credit?"

"Okay, but Randy had been there, at least. The clay figure proves it."

He didn't say anything.

"Let's look at the rest of the house and—"

My phone rang. It was Jakes.

"What are you up to?" he demanded.

"Hi, I love you, too."

"Alex . . ." I knew that tone.

"Okay, okay," I said. "George, Tonja and I went to a club tonight and met Patti—"

"What club? Why Tonja?"

"If you're going to interrupt me—"

"Forget it," he said. "Where are you? I'll come there."

"Um . . ."

He said, "Alex," again in that tone.

"We're at Patti's house."

"Your make-up artist?"

"Right."

"Is she there?"

"No."

"Who's we?"

"Me and George."

"Alex, put me on speaker." I pushed the little speaker icon. "Am I on speaker? Can you hear me, George?"

"I can hear you Jakes! How are you?" George answered sweetly.

"Did you break in?" I shook my head back and forth at George. "I know you're shaking your head, Alex. Did you, George?"

"No . . . well, not really. The door was open." George was doing his best not to lie. "But we found out something."

"Okay, you two," he said, wearily, "get out of there, right now. Go home. I'll meet you there."

"Okay, but—"

"Alex," he said, "we have no way of knowing where Sam Rockland's investigation is taking him. He could walk in on you."

"Oh . . . oooh, all right," I said. "I'll meet you at home."

"Fine. Oh, and Alex?"

"Yes."

"Don't take anything!"

Chapter 22

"But he said to leave!" George said, seconds later.

"Just a quick look around, George, and then we'll get out."

"Alex. What about Rockland? I don't want to get arrested. C'mon!" But I hurried away so that he had no choice but to follow me.

Patti had a room set up as an office, with a desk, a computer, a printer and more.

"Why does she have an office?" I asked.

"Everyone has a home office, Alex," George said. "We have one."

"Wayne's a screenwriter," I said. "He needs an office."

"Yeah, well," he reasoned, "students, housewives, retired people . . . like I said, everybody's got a home office, these days."

"I guess you're right." I didn't have one. Maybe I should get one, too.

George opened desk drawers, still using his shirt tail. "Look!" he said.

He'd opened a top drawer and there was a leather bound phone book. It had 2008/2009 embossed in gold on the cover.

"Let's have a look at it."

"What's the point? It's from three years ago."

"There might be something helpful in there."

"We can't leave our fingerprints on it, right? So how are we going to get it out of the drawer?"

"Very carefully."

I tried using two pens to pick the book up, but I had as much luck with that as I normally did trying to use chopsticks.

"Okay, wait," George said.

Once again he used his shirt tail covered hands and lifted the book out. I was able to turn the pages with my two pens.

"Whoa," I said, stopping when I got to the D's.

"What?"

"Look here, next to this name." I pointed with the pen I was holding.

Next to the name "Davina" was a fleur-de-lis, hand drawn in black marker. It was badly drawn, but I was able to recognize it.

"What is that?"

"It's a fleur-de-lis," I said.

"You really think so?" He squinted. "It looks like she used a black marker . . . it's kinda smudged . . . could be some kind of flower, I guess."

"Jeez, George." He questioned the clay animal, and now this.

"What do you think it means?"

"Probably that she met this person at the club. Look, there's an address and a phone number."

"The way that club's run," he wondered, "why would she have somebody's real address and phone number?"

"I don't know," I said, turning the page, "but there are more. Look, one in the F's, one in the J's."

I kept turning, kept finding more.

"Maybe certain people who met and liked each other exchanged personal information."

"That sounds like a good way to get killed," George said, then covered his mouth with both hands, hoping he hadn't just committed a *faux paux* and wished Patti dead.

"We don't have much time," I said.

"Oh, *now* you're concerned about time."

"I want to photograph these pages."

"You told Jakes you weren't going to take anything."

"Taking a photo is not the same thing as physically taking something, George."

"How can you do that without touching them?"

"There's got to be some kind of gloves around here somewhere. After all, Patti is a make-up artist."

"You're right! I'll check the kitchen," George rushed off, then returned with a pair of yellow rubber gloves. They weren't as thin as the ones Jakes carried in his pocket for handling evidence, but they were the kind that allowed the wearer to pick up a quarter.

I put them on and turned back to the D's. The phone book was a binder, so I was able to open it flat and lay it on top of the desk. I pulled out my cell phone and pushed the camera icon. God, I love my smart phone!

I photographed the D and F pages together, then the J's and the M's.
"All right," I said, "put the book back and let's get out of here."

The rain had increased, and soaked us as we ran to my Explorer. I made
sure the cell phone was safely tucked into my purse.

I wiped away water that was dripping from my nose. George was
wiping his face with both hands.

"Can you see?" he asked, as I started the car and turned on the windshield wipers.

"Don't worry," I said. "I'll get you home safe and sound."

Chapter 23

Heading out on Mulholland Highway to get back to the 10 Freeway was
all downhill. If we'd been driving on straight roads the problem may not
have materialized for a while. As it was, I knew we were in trouble immediately.

"We've got a problem!" I announced.

"What?"

"No brakes!"

"What?"

"The brakes aren't working!" I shouted.

George said something else but I concentrated on keeping the car on
the road through a turn.

"Don't crash," George said.

"I'm doing my best, George! Dial nine-one-one!" I shouted to my Blue
Tooth.

"Nine-one-one," a woman said. "What's your emergency."

George and I started talking at the same time.

"I can't understand you," the operator said.

"George! Shut up!"

"Ahhhh," he screamed as we went around a curve.

I told her where we were on Mulholland Highway and that we had
no brakes.

"Are you sure, Ma'am?"

"Yes, I'm sure!" I shouted.

"All right, I'll have someone try to intercept you."

"Lady, I . . . have . . . no . . . brakes! I need somebody to keep us from crashing."

"Where are you on Mulholland?" she said.

"We're a couple miles west of Cahuenga, before Laurel Canyon. Hello! Hello?" 911 wasn't saying anything. "A T and T dropped the call, George!"

"What are we supposed to do?" George shouted.

"I'm going to do the only thing I can," I said.

"What's that?"

"Slow down."

"How?"

I couldn't explain. My voice was starting to catch in my throat. Besides, I didn't know how. I had already taken my foot off the gas pedal. We were on a steep downhill and accelerating.

I remembered seeing a TV show about what to do in this kind of an emergency. I started pumping the brakes. That was supposed to work.

Nothing.

Low gear, I thought. Somebody had once told me you should switch into low gear. I did, but it didn't help at all.

Next I yanked on the emergency brake, but whoever had fiddled with my car had thought of that, too.

"George, you have to help me!" I shouted.

"How?"

"Keep searching up ahead for an uphill incline, some shrubbery, a field, something that'll slow us down," I told him.

"All I see is rain. I can't make out anything else!"

"There's got to be something else." If we struck a tree at this speed there was no telling how much damage there'd be.

Thank God it was late. We would have already been killed after starting a twenty-car pile up, but there was no one else on the road. The curves were the most dangerous thing, dropping off into dark nothingness on one side and smashing into huge jagged rocks jutting out on the other. It was dark, and the rain was coming down even harder.

Friction, I thought. I could scrape the car up against the guard rail until we stopped. Of course, if the guard rail gave way we'd fall off the road and into the canyon. But I had to do something; I didn't know how much longer I could keep the car on the road. If I drove directly into a guard rail it would give way for sure but if I could hit it at an angle we might have a chance.

"Hang on!" I said.

"What are you gonna do?" George demanded. "Can you even see?"

"Just barely," I said. The wipers were on high, but I could just make out the center line.

"I'm going to stop us, George!"

"How?"

"I'm going to use the guard rail."

"You'll kill us!"

"Just hold on!" I yelled.

"To what?" George asked, bracing himself.

The first impact wasn't so bad.

We struck the rail, and bounced off. It held. I hit it again, bounced, then hit it again. The next time we hit it we just kept scraping along, sparks flying.

"Oh my God!" George screamed.

Screeching metal, more sparks, and I felt the car start to slow down. If we could only stop before we ran out of guard rail, we might make it.

"Alex—"

"Hang on," I said, again. "It's working."

"Alex—"

"Shut up! I'm saving our lives!"

It seemed to go on forever and then, suddenly, we stopped.

George and I sat there quietly for a moment, before I realized we might not be out of the woods. The guard rail could still give.

"George! Get out. Get out!"

I opened my door, jumped out, slipped on the wet pavement and went down on my ass. George couldn't get out on his side because of the rail, so he slid over and looked down at me.

"Are you all right?" he asked.

"Yes, yes." I scrambled up and out of the way. "Get out!"

"Are you crazy!" someone yelled at me.

A man had gotten out of his car and was running toward me. I was trying to catch my breath when I saw his turquoise-tipped cowboy boots first.

"I'm sorry! No brakes! No brakes!" I gasped. It was all I could get out.

He stepped in closer as I looked up at him. He had on a large hat that kept me from seeing his face clearly. But I could see that he had long brown hair. I looked beyond him. There were no other cars stopping. In fact, at the moment there were no other cars on the road except for the stranger's Lincoln.

I looked back at the man. Something shiny was reflecting off of his hat.

"Are you all right?" He didn't sound exactly concerned, almost annoyed.

"Yes," I said, "yes. I'm, sorry. I'm so sorry. I had no brakes."

Suddenly there were flashing lights and two police cars pulled up.

"It could've been worse, lady. A lot worse," he said, and quickly disappeared.

Four young policemen jumped out of their cars and started asking questions, but all I could think to tell them was to call Detective Jakes.

Chapter 24

"George," Jakes said, as he arrived, "I would have expected better from you." He held his umbrella over me, but I was already soaked.

"W-why?"

Jakes looked at George and then at the condition of the Explorer. He turned to look at one of the uniforms.

"Didn't anyone call for an ambulance?"

"Yes, sir," the cop said, "but she sent it away."

Jakes looked at me.

"We're fine. Just a little shaken up."

"What happened?"

"We were headed home and the brakes gave out."

"Just like that?"

"I don't know," I said. "You tell me."

He frowned. "Could just be bad brakes. This didn't happen after the club, right? It happened after Patti's house."

"Maybe someone followed us."

"Did you see anyone?"

"No, but I wasn't looking."

Jakes looked at George.

"I didn't see anyone," George said. "But it's been raining so hard, you can barely see the road."

"Maybe you better go, George. I need to talk to Alex, alone." Jakes said.

"Are you and Wayne okay staying with Sarah a while longer?" I asked him.

"Sure. Take your time Sweetie. I could use a drink right now anyway. Do you have some wine at home?"

"Yes I do and you know where," I told him. "I'll be there soon."

"Okay," he said. He looked at Jakes. "You know you really shouldn't be mad at me. Just imagine what could have happened to Alex if I wasn't with her. I always have her back."

"I'm not mad, George. Just concerned, okay? I'll have a car take you home."

As he got into the police cruiser I heard him give the driver my address. It was good to know that he and Wayne would be there when I got home.

"What were you thinking?" Jakes asked me. "This time I should wring your neck."

"Just let me explain."

"I'll let you explain," he said, "but it should be someplace dry. Come on." He grabbed my hand.

"Where?"

"Someplace we can talk privately." He tugged me to his car, then stopped and looked at me. "Did you and Doctor Watson touch anything in Patti's house?"

I hedged. "Everything is the way we found it."

"And the front door?"

"What about it?" Jakes gave me the look I knew so well. "It wasn't locked, okay? That's the only reason we went in, to see if Patti was hurt."

"A likely story," he said. "Okay, come on."

He practically stuffed me into his car. My cell phone was burning a hole in my purse. I stole a quick look. Yep, the pictures were in tact.

Jakes decided to take me someplace very private—his apartment. We had put our heads together many times before in restaurants and bars, but this time he wanted no one else around us.

Jakes also arranged to have my car taken to the LAPD impound to be examined in the morning.

We stopped at a Starbucks to get two coffees. Jakes' kitchen was almost as clean as it had been when he first moved in. He took all his meals and drinks out.

We toweled off and sat down at his kitchen table and I told him about the club.

"Why didn't you call me before you went to there?" he asked.

"I didn't know if it meant anything," I said. "I mean, Patti just said

to meet her there. Besides . . . I didn't think you'd want to go to a club
. . . like that."

"Why not?"

"Well, you're kind of . . . straight."

"Of course I'm straight."

"No, I meant . . . straight-laced. You know . . ."

"Are you trying to say I'm too uptight to go to a swinger's club?"

"No, of course not," I lied. "I meant it's just not your . . . scene."

"But it's yours?"

"No," I said. "Look, we're getting off the point. I didn't want to call
until I knew I had something to tell you."

"And you do?"

"Yes," I said, "I have a lot to tell you, and then you can decide what
to do."

"Is that a fact?"

"Yeah," I said. "If you want to give this all to Rockland, that'll be up
to you."

He gave me a hard stare. "You know I don't want to give that asshole
anything," he said. "All right, talk. Impress me."

I told him everything that happened from meeting Patti at the door of
the club to calling him from her house.

"Let me see the clay animal you stole."

I took it out and passed it to him. "I didn't steal it," I said. "My daughter made it for her father."

He turned it over in his hands. "You say this is a dog?"

"It was made by a little girl!" I snapped. "Jeez, you're just like
George."

"Okay, take it easy," he said, passing it back. "You believe that office
belonged to Randy or, at least, that Randy spent time there?"

"Yes."

"I can check and see if Randy is listed as an owner of the club," he
said. "What else?"

"Patti," I said. "She's gone."

"Gone where?"

"I don't know," I said. "She ditched us at the club."

"Did she admit anything to you while she was there?"

"No," I said, "she was careful, except for the fact that she met Randy
at the club."

"Well, I know Rockland spoke with her, but I don't know if she's a
suspect or not. I'll see what I can find out."

"Have you talked to any of Randy's old clients?" I asked.

"I met with two of them, talked with another on the phone."

"And?"

"None of them seem to hold a grudge."

"That's amazing," I said. "He stole from them and they don't care?"

"They got their money back, Alex," he said. "In business that's pretty much all that matters."

"One of them might be lying."

"Hell, they all might be lying. But remember that's pretty much what we found out a while back, when Randy was still alive."

"Maybe somebody was planning to kill him later, and finally did."

"Maybe, but I don't think so."

"So there are no suspects?"

He hesitated.

"Jakes?"

"You'd be a suspect, but I can't see that you'd be a serious one. But then . . ."

"What?"

". . . Rockland's an asshole."

"Is he going to come after me?"

"He's probably going to want to talk to you again, at some point."

"If he doesn't come up with somebody better, he'll come after me, won't he?"

"Look, I'll do what I can, Alex. But you have to stay out of trouble."

"I will," I said, "but—

Chapter 25

"Now, don't get mad . . ." I said to him.

"Oh, that's never a good way to start a sentence," he said. "What did you do?"

"Well, while we waited for you, we looked around and . . ."

I told him about searching the house, which is how we knew Patti had packed and left. I also told him about looking through the desk, finding the old phone book and taking photos of some of the pages. I was careful to tell him that we used rubber gloves when handling the book, and put it back where we found it.

"Yeah, when you told me you left the place the way you found it I was afraid it was something like this," he said. "You know, our Forensics people are very good, Alex. If they looked hard enough they'll find some trace of you and George."

"Well," I said, lamely, "maybe they won't look so hard."

He sat there, shaking his head.

"Jakes?" I said. "You're not going to yell?"

"No," he said, "I'm not gonna yell. Let me see the photos."

I took my cell phone from my purse and handed it to him. He scrolled through the photos.

"How can you possibly see anything? Each shot is so tiny." I grabbed the phone from him.

"Here. You just widen out the image with your fingers. See? Streeeetch the image and it gets bigger. Gee, Jakes, it *is* two thousand eleven!"

He grabbed the phone back. After struggling with the screen for a minute, he managed to enlarge each one of the photos. "What did you say this mark is?"

"A fleur-de-lis."

"And that's a symbol the club uses?"

"Yes."

He squinted at the pages the way George had done.

"Maybe that's a little blurry—"

"No," he said, cutting me off. "It really doesn't matter what the symbol is. It's there, and it must mean something."

"We can check with those people," I said, anxiously, "see if they knew Randy—"

"Whoa," he said. "I think it's time for you to settle into the background."

"But . . . I'm the one who found this information."

"Alex—"

"Jakes, I can do things a cop can't," I said. "I can go places without needing a warrant—"

"—and that's called breaking the law!" he pointed out.

"Well . . . if you and I went together it wouldn't be breaking the law."

"No, I'd just get in trouble for messing with another detective's case."

"So what do you want to do?" I asked. "Give this information to Rockland? Or just let him try to build a case against me."

"Neither," he said, "that's not what I want to do."

"Look," I said, "there are men and women on that list. We can take turns. You talk to the women and I'll talk to the men."

"Why not the other way around?"

"Come on, Jakes," I said. "The women who go to those clubs will eat you up. Especially if you wear a uniform. Do you have one by the way?"

"Of course I do. And you're saying the men will love you?"

"Well, I'm not saying they'll love me, but I bet I could get them to talk to me more than you could."

He hesitated, still studying the photos.

"And if Rockland isn't going in this direction," I reasoned, "there's no chance we'll run into him."

"Unless," he said, "Randy also had a phone book with these names in it, similarly marked."

"I can probably find that out," I said. "After all, I'm the ex, the mother of his child. I'll bet I can get into his place."

"You'd have to go through Rockland for that," he said. "I could prob-ably—"

"No, let me do it," I said. "It makes sense. If you ask him, you're just going to tip him off to your involvement."

"You're probably right," he said.

"I'll call him and say I want to get into Randy's place because he has some of Sarah's stuff. Besides, the house isn't technically a crime scene, right?"

"Well, the back is still taped off, at the top and bottom of the hill. The house is an extension of that, but it's not sealed."

"Okay, then," I said. "I'll get in there and check Randy's phone book, and his computer."

"Do you need a key?" Jakes asked.

"Don't worry. I'll get in. I could go in without asking Rockland—"

"No," Jakes said. "Mention it to him. He'll probably say yes,"

"Okay," I said. "I'll call him."

"That'll be good. Not only could you match up some names from Patti's book, but you might find something in his computer that firmly connects him to the club. If he's even a part owner, that makes the other owners suspects."

"What if he owns it outright?"

"He still has to have some business associates," Jakes said. "It would also make club employees suspect."

"And once we collect all this information?"

"We may have to give it to Rockland," he said. "It depends on how much we want to risk my job and your freedom."

"My freedom?"

"If Rockland realizes you're butting your nose into his case, he may want to lock you up."

"Couldn't you keep him from doing that?"

He stared at me and said, "Not if I'm right in there with you."

That shut me up.

"All right," he said. "Keep these photos safe."

Jakes wanted me to stay the night but I told him I had to get back home to Sarah. And I had to work the next day. Except it was the same day now.

"What about Tonja?"

"I think she may have had it going on tonight," I said.

I got a blank look so I told him that Tonja had been familiar with the club and had insisted on going with us. She'd claimed she'd been to a club like that once, with an old boyfriend. But when we got there, it seemed she may have been more involved with that scene than she let on.

"For all I know," I finished, "she's still there. When we left she was kind of drunk and her skirt was on backwards."

I told him I had to get back to Sarah so Wayne and George could go home. "It's almost one o'clock. I have to be up in just a few hours. We gotta go."

"We don't know what went on with your car, and I don't think you should be alone tonight. I'll drive you and then I'm calling for a patrol car to stay in front of your house." Jakes grabbed his keys and ushered me towards the door.

"Oh, not that again! What will the neighbors say? They already must think I'm 'the crazy actress that lives down the lane'." This would not be the first time I'd had someone watching over me. I'd had cops parked on my street before when some lunatic had tried to run me off Pacific Coast Highway.

"I've got news for you, Babe. You *are* 'the crazy actress that lives down the lane.'"

I couldn't argue with that one so I just elbowed him in the stomach, threw my head back and walked out his door.

Chapter 26

When Jakes and I got to my house, George and Wayne were sitting in the living room drinking wine. George had a blanket wrapped around him. I assumed he had told Wayne about our misadventure. They both jumped up when we opened the door.

"Alex, are you okay?" Wayne asked as he hugged me. "Hello, Jakes. I don't blame you one minute for being furious with these two. They could have gotten themselves killed. Again!"

"I know, Wayne. Maybe you can talk some sense into George, cuz I don't seem to be having any luck with this one." Jakes put his arm around me and pulled me close. I smiled meekly. "Call if you need anything, okay? The cruiser should be here any minute. He's not going to come to your door or anything. He'll be very discreet." He kissed me and turned to Wayne and George, "I gotta get going. You be safe, okay, George? No more stupid stuff? 'Bye Wayne. Have a good night." He walked out just as the police car was pulling up. He exchanged some words with the cop and pointed to me. I waved at them then closed the door.

"Cruiser?" George and Wayne asked in unison.

"Yeah. We don't know for sure what was up with my car. It's no big deal. Just a precaution." I tried to sound blasé.

"You two are killing me! A precaution! How are you really doing, Alex? Really?" Wayne was in full mother hen mode.

"I'm hanging in there," I said in a very reassuring tone. "Any more of that wine left?"

"I'll get you a glass," Wayne said, "and then I want to hear everything."

He went to the kitchen and I looked at George.

"Are you really okay? That scared the shit out of me. How about you."

"Tell me about it, I'm still shaking. Do you really think someone was trying to kill us?" George's eyes were wide.

"I can't imagine why. We didn't do anything. Or find anything."

"Maybe it's that clay blob you took."

"Okay. It's a *dog*? And no one would want to kill us for that."

"You're right. Maybe it was just bad brakes in the rain, right? And you! I can't believe you managed to get the car stopped."

"I know. Don't ever underestimate the power of *Dateline on NBC.*" George looked confused. "I saw a show about what to do in case of different emergencies. Stopping out of control cars was one of them." I rubbed my face and sat next to him on the sofa. He shared his blanket with me. "Hey, is Sarah okay? I hope she's been sleeping."

"Wayne said she's been asleep since nine," he said. "Tonja's not home yet?"

"Her house is dark," I said. "What do you think? Is this going to be awkward, George? I mean, when I see her? She was like an alcoholic back on the booze tonight."

"So she was getting her freak on. Who cares?" George was being the voice of reason.

"I just hope it's not weird with us. She is my neighbor. We'll see, huh?"

Wayne returned with a glass of wine. We sat down and I told them about my conversation with Jakes.

"Are you and Jakes working together, trying to find out who killed Randy?" Wayne asked.

I nodded. "I really want to solve this for Sarah's sake, and mine, too. I can't do it without Jakes' help."

"He didn't read you the riot act for the business with the club?" George asked.

"That would be a yes," I said. "But not bad as riot acts go."

"So he's really not mad at me?"

"I don't think so."

George looked relieved. He liked Jakes and Jake's opinion matters to him.

"Wayne, thank you so much for watching Sarah," I said.

"Don't mention it, Sweetie," Wayne said. "She's so sweet. What a cutie."

George and Wayne finished their wine and then headed for the door.

"What about Patti?" George asked, as I walked them out.

"I don't know, George," I said. "I hope she's okay."

"Think she'll be at work tomorrow? Even with all her stuff gone?" George asked me.

"If her stuff is gone, she probably is too, right? I'd love to know why she ditched us. Maybe she just got scared."

"Scared of what?" Wayne interjected.

"Maybe she knows too much?" I wondered.

"What could she know?"

George and I looked at Wayne.

"Oh," he said, "you mean she might know who killed Randy!"

"That would be a good reason to leave town, wouldn't it?" George said.

"I don't like either one of you being involved in this one bit. Why can't your Jakes just take the case over and leave you out of it?" Wayne asked.

"I need answers. And besides, it doesn't work that way," I said. "It's Detective Rockland's case; he's in charge. He just doesn't know what we know."

"Then why not tell him?" Wayne asked.

"Jakes may have to, but they don't like each other, so . . ." I yawned and quickly covered my mouth. "Sorry!"

"You go to bed. I've gotta get some sleep, too," George said. "Some of us have to work tomorrow, even after a night of clubbing."

"Don't remind me of what could have happened to you, George. I'm still mad at you!" Wayne said.

"You're right to be mad. I shouldn't have dragged Georgie into this. It won't happen again." We exchanged hugs and kisses, I thanked them both and apologized to George.

"What for?" he asked.

"What for? For putting you in danger."

"You saved our lives," he said.

"And maybe I'm the one who almost cost you your life."

"A minor point," he said, giving me another hug. "Warm up and get some rest. Aren't you in bed tomorrow?"

"Don't remind me. And I will."

I watched from the door as they walked to their car. "Goodnight, officer! Keep my girl, safe!" I heard George say. He turned around and smiled at me. I smiled, waved, double-locked the door and went to have a hot bath.

Chapter 27

I was having coffee the next morning at about 6:30, feeling pretty crappy since I'd only had a few hours of restless sleep. I had been extremely amped up after last night's festivities.

I'd never heard from Tonja and was hoping she was okay. Maybe we'd made a mistake leaving her there by herself. What if something awful had happened to her? Something awful almost had happened to me and my explorer was out of commission because of it. I guess I'd have to take Sarah to school in my Porsche but there wasn't much room. Maybe I could ask the cop that was parked in front of my house. That wouldn't look so good, would it? My little girl being dropped off at school in a squad car? Then the doorbell rang. I opened it to Tonja.

"Good morning! How are you?" she asked me. "What's with the police car out front?"

"It's a long story. I'll tell you later. How are you?" I didn't really need to ask because she was still wearing her cowgirl outfit and looked like she had never gone to bed.

"Oh, I'm good. You said you didn't have to go to work early, right?" She was avoiding the obvious questions.

"No. You're fine. I have to be there at nine o'clock. Come in." I opened the door and she stepped inside reluctantly. "Coffee?" I asked.

"Oh God yes! Please! With cream and sugar." She sat down at the kitchen table while I poured her a cup. "Is Sarah still sleeping?"

"Yeah. I figured I'd get her up around seven. What happened to you last night, anyway?" I kind of knew all ready, of course.

Holding her head in her hands, she looked at me from between two fingers in front of her face.

"I had too much to drink. Ahh! Like I said, I ran into some friends and well . . . I had . . . fun."

"You seemed like you were having fun when we left you there." I didn't really need to know what kind of fun exactly and thought I'd leave that up to her to tell me. I handed her the coffee and placed a carton of half and half and a sugar bowl in front of her.

"Thank you, thank you." She poured some cream into her cup and a heaping spoon of sugar and took a sip. "Oh my gosh that's good."

I sat silently and waited. "Okay, look. I wasn't totally honest with you. I have been to those kinds of clubs before and I have done more than just, well, watch."

I gave her a look that said it all. Like I didn't know that?

"It had been a few years, though, since the last time I'd gone. Anyway, I hope you don't think less of me or anything?" She winced.

"Tonja, I don't care what you do in your personal life. I mean, as long as it's not drugs or anything dangerous. It's none of my business."

"Oh great!" She seemed genuinely relieved. "So did you, find anything? I mean, you know . . . what happened after I left you guys? What'd you do?"

"Uhhh, I wouldn't say it's necessarily for me, per se. Not really my thing, but whatever. You're okay? I was worried about you."

"I'm fine. Tired. I need a shower." She smiled. There was an awkward silence. I bet she did. "Did you, uh, find out anything about Randy last night? Anything helpful?"

"Not really," I lied. I figured it was best to keep her out of the loop from now on. Who knew who she hooked up with last night that might have known Randy? It was better to keep her out. The less she knew, the better.

"We didn't really find anything. Look, why don't you go home and get showered. I need to drive Sarah to school."

"Oh, yes, of course. Good idea." She got up and was heading out the door with the coffee in her hand. "Can I take this? I'll get the cup back to you."

"Sure. No worries. I'm glad you're okay."

"Thanks! See you!"

I stood at the window, watching her walk over to her house when she suddenly veered over to the patrol car. The cop lowered his window and she leaned in. They were talking for a few minutes. My God, does she ever stop? She backed up and waved to him as she went into her house.

I got my script out and looked at my lines. I was usually much more on top of it than I had been lately. Too preoccupied with other things, I guess. I didn't have too many lines, thank God. But I did have a love scene, which was a lot more work than most people would think. I should have probably gotten a spray tan. It always looks good on camera and saves the time of having to get make-up applied all over with a cold wet sponge. I probably could have used a few workouts at the gym, too. I looked in the mirror and pulled up my pajama top. Not much happening in the ab department. I turned around and looked at my butt. Yikes, those brownies had taken a toll. I had to admit that having had such a close call the night before really put things in perspective. Who cared about a little cellulite? I was happy to be alive.

I was reminded of this again when my adorable little girl came running out in her jammies.

"Hi Mommy! Can we have pancakes this morning?"

"Of course, we can. Come here, let me kiss you." I planted a big one on her cheek and squeezed her really tight. "I love you so much. Did you guys have fun last night?"

"We had a blast. Wayne's funny. We made s'mores in the fireplace."

"Really? The fireplace, huh?" I had visions of melted marshmallow all over the bricks.

"Can I help with the pancakes?"

"You betcha. Let's go."

We had a big pancake breakfast together then I took Sarah to school. Thankfully she didn't notice the cop car parked out front. I think she was too happy to be riding in Marilyn to notice. That saved me from having to explain what the police were doing in front of Mommy's house. I nodded to the cop as I pulled out of the garage.

My to-do list for the day had clicked in: drop Sarah off, jump into bed with someone I didn't know very well, avoid being killed. My life had officially gotten very weird.

Chapter 28

I had just pulled into the studio parking lot and was getting out of the car when George ran up to me.

"Patti's not here!"

"We figured that would be the case, right?"

"Yeah, but she quit *yesterday!*"

"How do you know?"

"Because Trudy said she got a letter of resignation from her yesterday morning." Trudy was the head of the WBN make-up department. It was for real.

I grabbed my bag and we started toward the Artist's Entrance, avoiding puddles along the way.

"That means she was planning on leaving before we went to the club last night."

"So what do you think, Alex? Do you think Patti knows more than she let on about Randy?"

"I don't know." We flashed our badges at Security and proceeded down the main hallway. "It could be she just couldn't handle us all knowing her secret life, ya know? I need to ask Jakes what he thinks." We headed up the elevator and got off on the first floor. I gave George a hug outside my dressing room door. "You okay, today?"

"Oh yeah. I'm fine. Pooped but fine. You?"

"I'm okay. Tonja came over this morning."

"Really? How was that?"

"Awkward. Sort of. She admitted she was more a part of that club life than she had said. No surprise there. I told her I don't really care what she does with her personal life. But I'm not sharing any more info about Randy with her."

"Smart. I better get back upstairs to make-up. I'll see you up there." He kissed me on the cheek. "You crazy girl!" Off he went.

I yelled after him. "Crazier than some. Definitely *not* as crazy as others."

He laughed.

"Spread your legs, Alex."

"Whoa, that's cold!"

"Sorry about that. I'm using warm water." Kathy replied.

Kathy was in charge of body make-up for the show and was used to actors complaining. We were at the end of the makeup and hair department, in the corner. There was a curtain drawn across the space so nobody could see us. Kathy was applying the make-up to my legs with a small sea sponge.

"How far up should I go? Did the director tell you what the shots are?"

"It's not HBO so not that far up, but she did say she wants legs. So . . . higher." I glanced down. "That's good." Then I looked at my chest. Okay, so I was a little vain. Call it an occupational hazard. "Could you give me some cleavage, Kathy? The girls need some oomphing."

"Sure. No problem." She turned back to the counter and dabbed a brush in dark powder. She applied it in between my boobs creating the illusion of cleavage. "There you go. Turn around and let me make sure there's no streaks."

She gave me the once over and handed me my robe. "You're good."

"Thanks, Kath." I started out the door and she stopped me.

"Hey, Alex. I saw Patti going into your dressing room yesterday. Did she tell you she was leaving?"

"No, she didn't. Did she tell you?"

"No. She'd been acting weird for a few days, though. We were close. So it kind of hurt my feelings she didn't at least say goodbye." Kathy turned back to her make-up counter.

"Oh, I'm so sorry. Maybe she'll call you, huh?" I patted her on the shoulder and left the room.

That was strange. I never knew Patti and Kathy were that close. How close was close? Did Kathy go to those clubs, too? I almost felt offended. Was everybody secretly swinging? Not that I'd necessarily *want* to go to the party but it would be nice to have be invited.

I didn't have time to ponder this new wrinkle. I had called Jakes as soon as I woke up and left a message telling him I was okay. But I needed to speak with him before I went out on stage. I wrapped my robe around me and sat down on the sofa, making sure not to smudge my body make-up. I called Jakes. He picked up on the first ring.

"I was just going to call you. Are you sitting down?"

"Yes. Why?" I asked.

"Your car was definitely tampered with. Someone cut your brake line."

"Oh my God! Someone tried to kill me! Do you know if they got any fingerprints?"

"The weather pretty much destroyed any evidence. What they did get was inconclusive." He took a deep breath. "Rockland knows about the brakes. And he knows that I put the cruiser on your house. He wants to see you."

"When?"

"He said he'd be in touch . . . personally," he answered.

"Patti isn't here, today. She gave her resignation yesterday. That means she planned on leaving before she brought me to that club." He was quiet on the line for a few seconds. I could tell something was up.

"Alex? We need to have a talk." Uh oh, I thought.

"What kind of talk?"

I finally asked.

"Later. In person."

I hated that later stuff. "Can you give me a hint?" I prodded.

"Alex to the set, please." Herbie's voice called out over the intercom, making me jump.

"Shoot! Jakes, I have to go. They need me. I'll call you when I'm done working, okay?"

"Okay."

I hesitated before hanging up, and so did he.

"Are we okay?"

"We'll talk later." And he hung up.

Something was definitely wrong but I didn't have time to think about it. I had some simulated lovemaking to do. I stood up, checked my make-up in the mirror and headed out the door.

Chapter 29

"Okay, Alex. I want you laying stage right in the bed and Marcus, you're stage left."

Sandy was our director again today. She pointed to the bed as I wrapped my robe around myself and adjusted my nude colored tube top, tugging it a little higher. I got into the bed and pulled the sheets up as I took my robe off. Some actresses did their love scenes topless. I never really got the point of that. This was pretend after all. And you couldn't show boobs on network television, anyway. I even had men's boxers over a pair of Spanx.

Marcus crawled into bed next to me. My character Felicia was still in the throes of amnesia. She had forgotten she was actually married to somebody else when she had fallen in love with Brandon (Marcus). Their relationship had caused lots of problems, considering Brandon was actually married to Felicia's daughter, Devon. I know. I have a hard time keeping up with it myself.

"Okay, so Alex," Sandy began, "the scene opens with you guys kissing. I want a nice long one. Two lovers that have this attraction that can't be stopped. Alex, make sure you're downstage." This meant she wanted to make sure the camera could see me. "I want to see the emotion all over your face. Then say your line. If you can get it going, a tear might be nice, too."

Great. I had to worry about flashing the crew, remembering my lines, showing my face, hiding my cellulite *and* now working myself up to tears.

"Then, Marcus, hold Alex's face in your hands and say your next line. Kiss again. Then when you pull apart, say your line about wanting to go back to Devon. That's where Alex slaps you."

"How do I slap him from this position? My arms will be pinned on the bed?" I asked. Doing a love scene was a lot like choreographing a dance sequence. Everything has to be just right so the scene works.

"Hmm. Good question." Sandy was thinking about this when Marcus piped in.

"How about if I pull her up to a sitting position when I break the second kiss and that way her arms will be free?"

"That should work. I'll make sure when I slap you that I just cross an inch in front of your nose, okay? Maybe pull back a little bit so I'll be sure to miss your face. And make sure you turn your head so it looks like a real slap. Like this." Marcus and I worked on the slapping a couple of times.

"That looks good," Sandy said. "Really sell that slap. Let's try it. We'll rehearse it first then give it a go. And Alex? Remember to hike the sheet up. We want to see some thigh."

Hooray. Thigh.

Sandy headed back to the booth where she could see the shots that all three cameras on the set were taking. The booth was where the show was put together, on the spot, and his several televisions across a wall. The Director, Producer, lighting people, sound people, production supervisors, even music people were back there making sure everything worked just right. The Director sat in front of the TVs and snapped her fingers when she wanted a specific camera to take a specific shot. A lot went into getting a scene.

Marcus and I were lying in each other's arms, waiting to start the camera rehearsal. It could be a little odd shooting the breeze when you're half naked in the arms of someone in a Speedo. But I guess I was more or less used to it.

"How are you doing today, Alex? How's Sarah?" Marcus asked me. He's a nice guy and a good actor. He had been a regular on The Depths of the Sea until its cancellation last year. There was definitely a glut on the market of out-of-work actors now that so many were being thrust into unemployment. Our show had hired quite a few. It was starting to feel like everyone from other defunct shows was jumping onto our ship. And our ship was the Titanic.

Marcus is actually a good kisser. Thank God. Nothing's worse than working with someone you don't like, let alone have to kiss them. As an added bonus, Marcus is very good looking. He's in his mid 30's (please don't call me a Cougar!), has brown hair and soulful hazel eyes. And a body that had helped him make it into *People Magazine's* 50 Most Beautiful People issue twice. He also has a girlfriend he's crazy about. He never tries to slip me the tongue and is always respectful. I love that about him.

"I'm okay, Marcus. Sarah's great. Thanks for asking. How about you?" Herbie walked over and interrupted us.

"Sandy wants to know if you guys can go straight to tape? We have a lot of scenes to do today and a five o'clock out time. You don't have much dialogue. Want to try it?"

Marcus and I looked at each other.

"Yeah, I'll try it. Alex?"

"Sure. Let's try it."

"They're the pros ladies and gentlemen!" Herbie said. He spoke into his headset. "Sandy, they said they'd do it."

Marcus and I assumed our positions. I adjusted my tube top, making sure nothing was showing.

"Make-up and hair? Final touch ups. Quickly!" Herbie yelled out.

George came running over and whispered in my ear.

"You look like shit today, Sweetie. Last night took its toll. Let's bring some of your hair in front. It makes you look softer."

"Shut up, George! I don't need to hear that now."

"You know I love you. I'm just trying to help. Add some lips." He grabbed the lip-gloss from the set make-up artist and dabbed some on my mouth.

"Thanks," I said, not meaning it. "Do you have any breath spray?" George reached into his pocket and pulled some out. I opened my mouth and he sprayed. Marcus opened his mouth up and George gave him some, too. I started thinking about the conversation I'd had with Jakes. He had sounded different somehow. Maybe he'd had it with my amateur sleuthing. He wouldn't break up with me, would he? Before I knew it I actually had tears in my eyes.

"We've got speed. Cameras rolling! Five, four, three, two . . ."

Marcus and I went into a kiss, making sure no bodily fluids were being exchanged. We pulled apart.

"I love you more than I've ever loved anyone," I said as Felicia. I squeezed my eyes closed and sure enough a single tear fell from my downstage eye. He held my face in his hands.

"How do you know if you can't remember anything?" Brandon asked.

"I know I'd remember feeling this if I ever had before." I looked into his hazel eyes and, grabbing him, pulled him into another kiss. This time there was just a little tongue. Oh well. It happens. Marcus pushed me away and pulled me into a semi sitting position.

"I can't do this, anymore. I do love you, Felicia. But what I have with Devon is different. It's deeper. She's my soul mate. I'm not getting a divorce. I'm not leaving Devon."

I looked at Marcus and noticed that someone had stepped directly into my eye line, off camera. As I pulled my arm back to slap Marcus I saw who it was.

Detective Sam Rockland was standing off to the side of the camera watching me. I lost my concentration and hauled off and slapped Marcus.

Chapter 30

"Damn! That hurt!" Marcus rubbed his cheek, working his jaw.

"Cut. That's a buy. Moving!" Herbie yelled out. "Good job you guys. One take. No rehearsal. Gotta love that! Hey, Marcus, you okay? She got you pretty good."

"I am so sorry, Marcus! I got distracted," I said looking around for Rockland. He was gone.

"I'm okay. I think," he said, still rubbing his face. I could see the imprint of my hand on his right cheek, even through his stage make-up. "You got a good left!" he added making light of it.

Andrea from wardrobe brought me my robe. I thanked her as I put it around me. As I jumped out of the bed, Sandy intercepted me.

"That was great! What a slap! Nice work, Alex. And Marcus. You really sold it," she said.

"Not too hard to sell that one," he answered, dryly. I started over to him but he held up his hand. "It's okay." Then he very slowly got out of bed and walked across the stage, opening and closing his mouth.

God, I felt bad, but where was Rockland? I headed off to my dressing room looking around behind the sets. Huh. No Rockland. I opened the door and there he sat on my sofa. I gasped.

"Hello, Alexis. Hope you don't mind me making myself at home?" My purse was lying on the coffee table in front of him. My cell phone was in it.

"Not at all, Detective," I said as I grabbed my purse and brought it over to my make-up counter. "Give me a second and let me put my clothes on." I closed the door that divided the main dressing room from the make-up area and quickly put my street clothes on. After running my fingers through my hair and collecting myself, I slid the door open.

"Interesting job you have. Do you enjoy it?" he asked as he scooted over on the sofa, making room for me. "Please, have a seat."

I opted to sit on the chair across from him. "Oh, you know. It has its positives and its negatives. Like any job."

"From what I saw, it's definitely not like 'any' job." He smirked. There was something about him that made me want to try my slap out again.

"So. What can I do for you, Detective?"

"You can try telling me what the hell you've been up to?"

"I don't know what you mean." Yeah, I did.

"You and your boyfriend have been involving your selves in my case," Rockland said.

"My boyfriend?" I didn't know if he was making a snide remark about George, or actually talking about Jakes.

"I heard you had some car trouble," he said. "Bad brakes? On no, wait, somebody deliberately messed with your brakes. Right?"

"I'm really not sure what happened."

"Well, then I'll tell you what happened. Somebody tried to kill you and your friend George last night on Mulholland Highway. So why would that be?" he asked. "Why would somebody want to take you two out?"

"I honestly don't know." I was shaking my head then I looked at him and added dryly, "Maybe somebody doesn't like my acting."

He sat forward and glared at me. The polite policeman was gone. "I don't need you and *Detective* Jakes messing up my case, Ms. Peterson," he said. "I heard you went to a club with Patti Dennis, and now she's missing."

"What's Patti got to do with anything?"

"Don't play dumb with me, Alex," he said. "She was a witness, and now she's gone after spending time with you. And somebody tried to kill you. I'd think you'd want to help me, not get in my way."

"I do want to help," I said. "What can I do?"

"What'd Patti tell you about your ex husband's death?" he asked.

"Nothing," I said. "She took me to a club she thought I might be interested in. I wasn't."

"That's it?"

"That's it."

"And you didn't know she knew Randy, and that he's involved with the club?"

"Involved how?" I asked.

Rockland just sat there biting away at his lower lip. It seemed like he was trying to figure out how much I knew about Randy and Trois ou Plus.

"Are you telling me he got into the swinging lifestyle?" I asked, giving him the most shocked expression I could muster. "Randy was never into that kind of thing when we were married. I can't believe he would ever be interested. Why would you think that about him? It's just so not him!"

He sat back again, studying me. Did he already know that Randy was a partner in the club? Or, at least, that he was involved?

"Jakes put a car on your house because of your close call on Mulholland?" he asked.

"I don't know. Maybe he thinks I'm cheating on him," I suggested. "Why don't you ask him?"

"That's funny," he said. He stood up, buttoned his jacket. "You better watch your step, Alex, or you'll get in trouble, just like your boyfriend did."

"What kind of trouble?" I asked. "What are you talking about?"

"You didn't know?" he asked. "Detective Jakes got called on the carpet for interfering with my case. By now he's probably on administrative leave—if he hasn't been busted back down to directing traffic."

"What do you—"

"Just remember," Rockland said, "keep your nose out of my case."

"Hold on," I said, standing up.

He stopped, halfway out the door. "Yeah?"

"I need to get into Randy's house."

He stared at me as if I had just sprouted horns. "Didn't you hear anything I just said?" he asked. "Stay out of—"

"Look, Randy was my daughter's father, and there are some toys and clothes in the house that belong to her. Now, his house is not a crime scene. He didn't die there, so I really don't need your permission, but I thought I'd ask. You know, just to be open and honest with you."

He stared at me for a few seconds, then said, "Okay, go ahead. Do you need a key?"

"He gave me one in case of an emergency," Technically, that wasn't true. But I had a strong feeling I would be able to find a key at the house. I didn't want to take anything from Rockland, anyway.

"Just take what belongs to your daughter," he warned.

"Of course."

Chapter 31

As soon as Rockland left I called Jakes.

"Rockland just left."

"Was he polite?"

"Not exactly polite. The more I see of him the more I don't like him," I said. "He told me you'd been called on the carpet. Is that what you want to talk to me about?"

"Yes."

"What happened?"

"Let's meet."

"You don't sound like yourself. What's going on?"

He ignored my question. "You're still at work, right? So am I. Are you comfortable with meeting at the Grove?" The Grove is an outdoor shopping mall just a few steps from the studio's back entrance.

"Sure. That was quite a while ago." Two lunatics had tried to kill George and me at the dancing fountains at the Grove a year earlier. "On second thought, maybe we should make it The Farmer's Market, next door. I'll get a little grocery shopping done." That's me. Queen of the multi-taskers.

"Okay, let's meet at Dupar's in twenty minutes."

"I'll see you soon, Jakes. I—" But he hung up. Had he actually hung up on me? Something was wrong. Very wrong.

I rushed a quick shower to get my body make-up off and threw my street clothes back on. I could have just walked over to the Farmer's Market but it was starting to pour again. I took my car, literally about 100 yards to the parking lot next door. Even through the rain I could see Jakes waiting for me at a table inside the restaurant. He didn't look happy. I pulled into a spot as close to the door as possible, turned off my engine and not even bothering with an umbrella, I made a run for it.

"So, what's going on?" I asked as I approached his table. I took off my coat and shook it. "You're in trouble?"

"Yes. Sit down."

"He said something about you being put on administrative leave," I sat.

"I have been." He wasn't looking at me, just stirring his coffee with a spoon.

"What's that mean, exactly?"

"It's like being suspended."

"I'm sorry," I said. "This is because of me?"

"It's not that simple."

"What's not?"

"It's not just about you and what you're doing or not doing."

I was trying hard to follow what he was saying but I was already lost.

"Jakes, what the hell is going on?" I finally said.

"Something's up with Rockland. He has it in for me. I never should have been put on administrative leave just for putting a car at your house. Not with the years I have and my record." Jakes was clearly worked up.

"Sooo, what do you think's going on?"

"I'm not sure, but it's pissing me off. It feels personal."

We sat quietly for a few moments.

"What do you want to do?"

"I want to walk." He abruptly got up and left a five on the table. "Walk with me?"

"Of course." I stood up and went to hug him. He hugged me back but it seemed perfunctory. "Hey! C'mon, Jakes. What's up with you?" I put my hands on his face and kissed him. "I've never seen you like this before." He took my hands in his and squeezed them before letting them go.

"I'm out of sorts, Alex. Let's walk." And he headed out the back door toward the covered section of Farmer's Market. Any thought about getting some groceries had left me as I tried to figure out what was going on with Jakes. He stopped in front of the Butcher section near a string of sausages hanging from the ceiling, and looked around.

"What happened when you asked Rockland about going into Randy's place?" he asked.

"He wasn't thrilled. But I explained how Sarah had some toys and clothes still there."

"How was his attitude toward you?" He started walking again.

This time I stopped in front of a candy counter and turned to him. "He was an ass. Kind of condescending and just sort of rude." Jakes was nodding as we headed over to the French gourmet display. "After Rockland left I started thinking about something."

"What?"

"Well, he said he knew I went to the club with Patti," I said. "He also said maybe I had something to do with her leaving."

"What did you say?"

"I tried to play dumb," I said. "I think he saw right through me. Something was kind of creepy."

"What?"

"How did Detective Rockland know I went out with Patti?"

"I don't know," he said. "Maybe he has somebody watching the club and they recognized you."

"Can you find out?"

"It might be hard since I'm on leave," he said, "but I'll do it. Are you ready to go over to Randy's, now?"

"But, what about—"

"Since I'm on leave," he said, "Rockland can shove it."

"You mean . . . you're still going to help me?"

"I'm not just helping. I'm going to solve this. Rockland made it personal and I'm taking it that way."

"But, if you get caught—"

"Let me worry about that," he said.

Chapter 32

Jakes had followed me over to Randy's house in his car. I had to pick up Sarah from school soon. Every time I looked in the rear view mirror, he had a distracted and intense look on his face. I had never seen Jakes like this before and frankly, didn't know how to deal with it.

I pulled up in front of Randy's house and cut the engine. I didn't make a move to get out. I was a little afraid of this new Jakes. He knocked on my window.

"Yeah?" I said as I lowered it.

"Ready?"

"No. I'm not. Are we okay, Jakes? Because something feels different and I'm not sure what it is." I surprised myself with tears. I quickly wiped them away. I didn't like feeling this vulnerable.

"We're . . . okay. I just need to figure some things out." Figure some things out? I didn't like the sound of that but before I could say anything he opened my door.

"Ready?"

No, I wasn't but I got out of the car anyway.

We walked to the front door. Randy's house wasn't too aesthetically pleasing. It had to have been built in the eighties and even the exterior reeked of bachelor circa 1985. I guess I expected some yellow police tape, or a police seal on the door, but there was nothing. Most likely that was because the actual murder took place in the backyard, and cops had taken whatever they wanted or needed from the house, already.

"Do you have a key?" Jakes asked.

"No, but I think I know where one is."

Randy was a horrible husband, a thief and apparently a swinger. He was also a creature of habit. I looked around the yard and saw several large rocks. One looked a little different from the rest. I walked over to it and picked it up. Sure enough there was a nice shiny house key lying on the ground under it.

"How did you know it was there?" Even in his bad mood Jakes couldn't help but smile a little.

"He always used to have a hide-a-key rock like this when we lived together. I figured he still would." I wanted to say he never had any imagination, but he had enough to steal, didn't he?

I tossed Jakes the key and let him open the door. He handed it back to me as we stepped inside.

"Do you know your way around?" he asked.

"Sort of. I checked the place out once to make sure it was safe for Sarah to be here."

We left the entry foyer and went into the living room.

"I don't have to worry about fingerprints, do I?" I asked.

"Probably not, but let's wear gloves, anyway." He took two pairs of latex gloves from his pocket and passed me one.

"Okay," he said, "I don't think there's any point in searching this room, or the kitchen. Let's do his bedroom. Is there a home office?"

"Yeah. Straight down this hallway and to the left."

We walked down the hall and came to the bedroom, first.

"I'll take the bedroom and you take the office." Jakes said.

"Okay." And I headed down the hall and took a left.

It was a big room with a large desk and a bunch of file cabinets. I walked over to the desk and could see, from the dust marks, that a computer had been there. It was gone now. I opened the cabinet drawers and it was obvious someone had taken several files out of there, too. I turned toward the closet and saw a large 8 x 10 photo of Randy and Sarah hanging on the wall. It had been recently taken from the looks of it. I hadn't realized how much Sarah favored her father until I saw the picture of the two of them, together. There was a window overlooking the back of the house. I looked out at some yellow police tape flapping in the wind and rain, then turned away.

There was nothing in the closet of any consequence. Just some old clothes and office equipment. I headed back to the desk.

There were three drawers on the left, three on the right, and one right in the center. The top three drawers across were all shallow, holding mostly pens, paper clips, small pads of paper, rubber bands, tape, scissors, rulers—supplies you'd find in most desks. The rest of the drawers were deeper.

Jakes entered the room and said, "Find anything?"

"Nope. Computer was taken. I'm assuming by the police. The filing cabinet drawers are empty.

"I'll go through the desk drawers." He crouched down next to me to look in the drawers on one side. I was reminded of just how much I liked the way he smelled.

"So you haven't found anything at all? Not even a phone book?" he asked.

"Nope."

He switched to the other side and started going through drawers.

"I didn't see anything that had to do with the club," I said.

"No, me, neither," he said. "Nothing with a fleur-de-lis on it." He looked exasperated. "This is a bust. Nothing. Let's get out of here."

"Wait," I said, as we left the office.

"What?"

"I told Rockland I'd be picking up some of Sarah's things," I reminded him. "I really would like to do that."

"Then we better do that."

We reversed direction in the hall, went past Randy's room and found the one he had set up for Sarah. I was shocked. It was really cute. Randy had gone to a lot of trouble for his daughter since the last time I had been here. He obviously had planned on staying in her life. It made me like him a little more. He had gotten her a four poster bed with a gauzy canopy hanging overhead. Everything was in pinks and purples. It was sweet . . . really sweet. He even had a matching dresser and a little desk with a box of markers and a coloring book on it. A flat screen TV was on the wall next to the window and some DVDs were stacked under it. It looked like Randy had gotten her the Disney classics, the Shrek movies, even *How to Train your Dragon* and *Tangled*.

"Wow. We can't take all that."

"We'll just take what we can." I glanced at a clock by her bed. "I have to get Sarah, soon. Could you find me a box? Please?"

"Okay," he said. "A box."

I collected a few toys and stuffed animals I knew I didn't have for her at my place. I also grabbed a cute sweater and the DVDs under the flat screen. What was taking Jakes so long to find a box? Everybody has boxes in their house, don't they? Maybe in a pantry or something?

I left the room, went down the hall. "Jakes?"

No answer.

"Jakes! Where are you?" I called, louder.

I started to walk a little faster, looking for the kitchen. Something felt off. Maybe it was just the fact that today had been so weird. He was probably fine, had probably stepped outside for a minute, but still . . .

I found the kitchen.

Jakes was lying on the floor, his blood staining the blue-tiled floor.

"Jakes!"

I rushed to him, becoming aware too late that someone else was in the room. I started to turn, and then something hit me. Before the lights went out I looked down and saw turquoise-tipped cowboy boots . . .

Chapter 33

I opened my eyes and looked up at Jakes. He had blood on his forehead.

"What?" I asked.

"Take it easy, Alex," he said. "We both got hit from behind."

I realized I was lying with my head in his lap. He was holding a gun in his right hand.

"Are you okay?" I asked.

"Yes," he said. "I came to a few minutes ago. How do you feel?"

"I have a headache."

"Me, too, but you have a bump, no cuts. Do you feel like standing?"

"No," I said, "but let's give it a try." He started to help me up, but I stopped. "Wait! What time is it?" I asked.

"Ten to two."

"I have to get Sarah at two forty-five."

He helped me to my feet gently. I thought I'd get dizzy, but I didn't.

"Where'd he go?"

"Don't know."

"Should we look for him?"

"Not 'we'." He looked out the window. I looked at his gun.

"I thought they took your gun away?"

"My service gun, but I had my off duty gun, here." He pulled up his pants leg and showed me his ankle holster. "I don't have anything to identify myself as a police officer, though."

"Jakes, who would be in Randy's house and why would they want to knock us out?"

"Could be a burglar, I guess, who saw Randy's obit in the paper." We looked at each other skeptically.

"So he just happened to come along the same time we did?"

"Apparently."

"Kind of a coincidence, right?"

"Yeah, too much of one." Jakes said.

A drop of blood dripped from just above his eyebrow to the floor.

"I should take care of that."

"First let's find out if he's still here," he said. "Stay behind me."

We crept through the house, Jakes with his gun held ready, but we didn't find anyone in any of the rooms.

"He's gone," Jakes said, lowering his gun.

"What did he take?"

"Let's look around."

We didn't see anything obviously missing.

"There was some jewelry in the bedroom, and some cash."

We went to the master bedroom and he showed me. It was all still there.

"Why would somebody break in and not take anything?" I asked.

"Maybe because . . ."

"Because . . . what?"

"I don't know," he said, "maybe someone's trying to scare us. Or warn us. I have a feeling we should get out of here."

"Let's go to the bathroom. I'll clean your head, and then we gotta go." Jake's brow was furrowed. "What's wrong, I mean besides the obvious?"

He put his gun back in his ankle holster. Shaking his head he walked into the bathroom with me behind him.

"Don't like it."

We found a box in a closet off the kitchen.

"Thanks," I said, still trying to get a read on him. He was a sphinx. I took the box. It was big enough. I set it on the floor and placed the toys and animals from the bed into it. I threw the sweater in, too. They fit with room to spare so I grabbed all the DVDs and put them in, as well.

"That it?" he asked.

"Pretty much."

He picked it up and said, "Let's get out of here."

We went out the front door. Jakes handed me the box and I hurried to Marilyn.

"Call me later, okay? We need to talk."

I wanted to talk right now but I had to get Sarah. I started to get into my car, but I was too late.

A siren started to whoop, and there were flashing lights behind us.

We were busted.

Jakes walked over and joined me by my car. He turned away from the officers and faced me.

"I don't want to identify myself if I don't have to."

"I understand," I said. "You don't need any more trouble. Besides, you can't prove you're a cop, and you have a gun on you."

"Yes," he said. "None of this is good news."

Two uniformed cops got out of the cruiser and walked up to our cars, one on each side. They had their hands on their belts. They both looked like they were still in high school. I mentally named them "Young and Younger". "Younger" actually had an extra stripe, which put him in charge.

"Ma'am, do you have some identification, please?" he asked.

"Of course." I gave him my driver's license, noticing that his nametag said Simpson. The other cop's tag said Hailey.

"This is not your house," he said, "yet you came out carrying a box."

"Yes," I said. "The house belongs to my ex-husband. I was picking up some things that belong to our daughter. As a matter of fact, she's going to be getting out of school very soon, and I need to pick her up."

"Well you'll just have to hold on," Officer Simpson said. "We got a call from someone who said they saw someone suspicious loitering by the side of the house. Were you two outside for any reason?"

"Who would want to be outside in this weather?" I gestured to the sky and of course it was clear as a bell. "Well, you know what I mean. It's been raining pretty much all day."

Jakes jumped in. "Officers, we came to retrieve her little girl's possessions and that was it. Just what's in the box she carried out?"

"Can you both step away from the car, please?" he asked.

Great. If they searched us they'd find Jakes' gun. Then he'd have to explain who he was, and have to prove it.

"Sir," Officer Hailey said, "your head is bleeding."

"Oh, yeah," Jakes said, touching his wound. "I . . . hit it when we were in the house. An accident."

"Please," Hailey said, "both of you, put your hands on the car."

We obeyed.

Simpson leaned in and looked in the box.

"Whataya got?" Hailey asked.

"Toys."

"That's it?"

"Yup."

"The house belongs to Randy Moore," Simpson said. "Your name is

... Alexis Petersen." He read it off my license.

"Yes," I said. "We were married; I just never took his name. Look, I really have to get my daughter!"

"Wait a minute," Hailey said. "I know her."

"What?" Simpson asked.

"Yeah, now that you said her name," the other man said. He looked at me, smiling. "You're on the *Bare and the Brazen.*"

"That's right."

"Wow," he said, "wow, I'm a big fan."

"Oh, no," Simpson said. "Not your soap operas."

"Only the best soap opera," Hailey said. "And she's Felicia."

"Felicia," Simpson said, staring at me with a bored expression.

"Hi," I said, with an anxious smile.

"I think we should pat them down," Simpson said. "Maybe they took something else."

"But why?" Hailey said. "I told you who she is."

"Yeah, well, if Lindsay Lohan can steal a necklace, I guess a soap opera star can steal something, too."

Oh my God, I thought, he just compared me to Lindsay Lohan!

Chapter 34

I was in my car driving to Sarah's school five minutes later. The two cops halfheartedly frisked both of us, but didn't search the car. Officer Hailey's fan-boy geek-out continued to get worse until his partner got tired of it and gave up. They wished us both a good day, then returned to their cruiser.

My Bluetooth sang out, "Jakes!" My heart skipped a beat.

"How's your head?" I asked. I really wanted to ask if his foul mood had lightened up but I thought I'd hold off.

"Fine. How's yours?"

"Fine." There was just a moment of awkward silence. What, us?

"We were lucky we ran into a fan," Jakes said. "Otherwise those two might have actually done their jobs and found my gun. Then I would have had a lot of explaining to do."

"I'm sorry I got you into this mess, Jakes," I said.

"You haven't gotten me into any mess, Alex," he said. "It's your ex-husband's fault for getting himself murdered. Knowing how much you want to get answers for Sarah I can't very well just sit by and do nothing."

"Maybe," I said, "but I don't expect you to risk your job for me—"

"Let's forget that for now," he said. "I told you, Rockland has made this very personal for me."

"I'm pulling up at Sarah's school. Call me later?"

"You do that while I go and try to get a few questions answered.

"Like how Rockland knew I went to the club?"

"Yes, and who made the call about somebody breaking into Randy's house."

"How can you find that out if you're on leave?"

"I still have friends there, who owe me favors," he said, "I'll call you later when I know something."

"Call me even if you don't know anything." There was another awkward pause.

"Alex?"

"Yes?" I found myself holding my breath.

"I can't have a cruiser out front anymore, but I think if somebody was trying to kill you they had a chance to get it done today."

"So you don't think I'm in danger?"

"Maybe not of getting killed," he said, "but I don't even want you to get another knock on the head, so I'm going to see if I can get a friend of mine to keep an eye on you. Remember Harry Slattery? He'll do it."

"How without Rockland knowing?"

"Screw Rockland." he said. "But don't worry about it. You won't even see him. I'll call you."

He hung up.

And he hadn't said, "I love you."

After Sarah and I got back home, I waited for her to get in the house before I pulled out the box of toys from Randy's. I still hadn't told her about her father's death and didn't want any difficult questions, like: "why do we have her things from Daddy?" or "why haven't I seen Dad lately?" I put the box in the hall closet and went to fix Sarah a snack.

I was making peanut butter crackers as I went through the day in my head. I kind of felt the same way Jakes did. If the man at Randy's house had wanted to kill us, he would have. Tampering with my brakes could have killed both George and me, but maybe it was just done it scare us. Killing us—or me—did not seem to be anybody's priority, yet.

And thinking about Mulholland made me remember the cowboy boots. The man who had approached me after our brakes failed and we crashed, had worn them! So had the man at Randy's! And the guy on the road had said, "It could have been worse." Suddenly, those words sounded very menacing.

I grabbed my cell phone and a jacket and went outside, out of Sarah's earshot. The rain had stopped so I sat down in a lawn chair on the dock and called Jakes.

"You called me on your cell, where are you?" he asked before I could say anything.

"I'm outside. I didn't want Sarah to hear."

"Oh. Okay. What's up?"

I really didn't like his tone and almost told him to screw himself, but thought better of it. I told him what I had remembered.

"That links the car together with whoever hit us, don't you think?" I asked.

"If your memory is right, I'd say so."

"There was no break-in at Randy's, right?"

"Right," he said.

"So did we leave the front door open? Is that how they got in," he said.

"No way. I made sure to lock it behind us when we were inside."

"Somebody must have had a key."

"Somebody who was involved with Randy," I agreed.

"Okay," he said, "let me do some research into this guy with the turquoise-tipped cowboy boots. I'll talk to you tomorrow."

"Wait a minute! Don't hang up. What is going on with you? Why won't you talk to me?"

He was quiet for a second.

"I guess I don't know what to say right now. I just . . ." pausing he added, "let me call you right back."

"Wait!" But he had hung up. I just glared at my cell. Then my phone rang. My house phone. I ran inside and it was Jakes.

"Why are you calling me on this phone. What is happening?"

"I'm sorry to do this, Alex. I just need some time. I think we need a break."

"What? You want a break? Why?"

"I know it sounds stupid. I feel like my life is at a standstill. Maybe it's a mid-life thing."

"So go get a Porsche. I'll loan you mine! A standstill? How do you figure? You've got a great job. Well, I mean you will again. And you've got me. You know."

"I'll talk to you about it soon."

"Jakes wait. This feels so sudden. What happened?"

He was quiet until I heard a long sigh. "I feel like life is passing me by. It sounds silly even saying it."

"What? How could . . ."

"I promise we'll talk. Just not right now. It's been a long day. You did good, Alex. Why don't you get some rest and we'll talk tomorrow. Goodnight."

And he hung up.

Without saying I love you. Again.

"Love you, too, Jakes."

After I hung up I started furiously making more peanut butter crackers until I realized I'd made about 40. I put one in my mouth and wiped away a tear. Pretty soon I was really crying and Saltine cracker crumbs were spewing from my mouth.

"Mommy? What's wrong?"

Chapter 35

"What's wrong, Mom?" Sarah had wrapped her arms around me. She looked up and she had tears in her eyes.

"Nothing, Honey." That was stupid. Anyone would know something was wrong here. "Well, actually Jakes and I had a little fight. That's all. It'll be okay."

"Are you guys gonna break up, too?" Oh, God!

I sat her down on the sofa. "I don't think so, Sarah. I really don't." What if we did? I took a breath. "But even if we did you know you and I will always be alright, right? You're my happiness and my number one girl. You know that, right?"

"Yeah. But, Mom? I really like Jakes."

"I do too! And honey he loves us. Don't you worry about Mommy and Jakes." I gave her an extra big hug. "Now it's just us girls tonight. What do you want to do after dinner? Manicures and facials? Oh, I know. Draw Grandma a picture, maybe?"

"I already drew her one last week."

"Okaaay." I thought about it for a second. We needed a distraction. "What about a movie night? We haven't had one in a long time!"

"Hooray! Let's watch a movie! With popcorn, and hot chocolate, too?"

"Yeah, why not? Go in your room and get started on your homework. I'll come and help you in a few minutes." I gave her a hug and swatted her on the fanny. She ran out of the room.

I looked out at the canal. The rain was still falling, the ducks were still gliding across the water. Life goes on and I wasn't about to let my love life screw up my daughter's life, again. I wiped away my tears (and a few crumbs), got up and started dinner.

It was dark out. I went around the house and made sure all the windows and doors were tightly locked. I looked out the front window and noticed a Toyota parked across from the house. That must be Harry. He was wearing a hat so I couldn't see his face clearly. He saw me and waved. I waved back. Harry is an old friend of Jakes that had left the department a long time ago. I had to admit I did feel better having someone watching over us.

"What movie do you want to see, Mommy?" Sarah had her jams on and had piled her favorite blankets on the floor of the living room.

I turned away from the window and crossed to the sofa.

"I don't care. It's your call, Sweetie."

"I've already seen all our movies, Mom, about a hundred times."

"Is there anything on TV? Anything we TIVO'd?"

She pushed the LIST button on the remote. "No. Just a bunch of *Sponge-Bob* episodes and *Hannah Montanas.*"

"Look in your cupboard one more time." She ran back to her room to give it another try. Then I remembered the DVDs I had gotten from Randy's! I went to the closet, pulled out the box and found *Tangled, Shrek Forever* and *How to Train Your Dragon.*

"Surprise!" I yelled when Sarah came back into the room empty-handed.

"Oh, awesome Mom! Where did you get those? Daddy has them at his house, too."

"Really, Honey?" I didn't want to lie to her and wondered if I should just bite the bullet and tell her about her father.

She beat me to it.

"How come Dad hasn't called me? He said he was taking me to the Santa Monica Pier soon."

"Sarah, come sit next to me." She walked over and we sat on the sofa. I put my arm around her and held her close for a minute. Then I pulled away from her and looked her in the eyes. "Honey, I have something sad to tell you."

"What is it? Did Dad leave again, Mommy?"

"No, no. Well no, not like before, Sweetheart." I was really struggling. "You know Dad had his problems, right? He left us a long time ago. But he never ever *ever* stopped loving you. In fact, I know for sure he loves you more than anything else in the whole world." Sarah was looking at me with such an earnest expression I started to tear up.

"What's wrong, Mommy?"

"Oh Honey, what happened is . . . Daddy's in heaven. He had an accident and was hurt. The doctor couldn't help him and he went to heaven."

"He died?" I nodded and pulled her closer. I could tell she was trying hard to process this huge information. "Did it hurt?"

"I don't think he was in pain, Honey. No."

She had a thoughtful look on her face. "So he's with Grandpop?"

"Yeah! Your Dad is with my Dad."

She hugged me tightly and started to cry.

"I'll miss him, Mommy. I liked having Dad back."

"I know, Honey. I'm so sorry. He's still around you, you know? He's your own very own guardian Angel. Just like I talk to my Dad sometimes? You can still talk to your Dad, too. Now you've got two angels watching over you and keeping you safe."

She wiped her eyes. "Yeah, Mom. And now Grandpop has someone to keep him company."

"That's right, he does." We sat like that for awhile, not speaking while I rubbed her back. I guess she was trying to figure out what it all meant. "Do you want to ask me anything or talk about it some more? We don't have to have a movie night if you don't feel like it now."

"No, Daddy got me those movies. I'd like to watch one."

"Which one?"

"Ummmm. *Shrek Forever.*"

"Okay. Shrek it is." I started to pull the disc out of the box.

"I wanna do it, Mommy!"

"So I gave it to her and she ran over to the DVD player and put it in the disc tray.

"Nothing's happening."

"Did you push PLAY?"

"Yeah. What's wrong with it?"

I walked over and fiddled with the buttons, took out the disc and reinserted it. Still nothing. I pushed EJECT and pulled out the disc again and looked at it. It didn't have anything on it. No picture of Shrek, no information about the movie. It was in the Shrek box but it wasn't the movie.

"I don't know, Sweetie. Let's try another movie."

She popped in *How to Train Your Dragon*. Same thing. Nothing. I looked at that disc and it was blank, too. Nothing on it. Strange.

I opened up the *Tangled* box; there was artwork on that disc. Sure enough, I put it in the player and voila! We were in business.

"Yay! I wanted to see *Tangled* when it came out, remember, Mom?"

"I do. Come here." We snuggled into the blankets on the floor and put the bowl of popcorn between us. We were only fifteen minutes into the movie when I looked over at Sarah and realized she was sleeping. I guess sometimes sleep is the best way to deal with something sad. I quietly untangled myself from the blankets, picked her up and put her into her bed.

I walked back into the living room and started to fold the blankets and put away the popcorn bowl and cocoa mugs. I hoped I'd handled telling Sarah about her Dad in the right way.

As I was cleaning up, I found the two discs with nothing on them. Just on a hunch I brought my computer over to the sofa and put in one.

At first it looked like it was blank. But I left it in for a few seconds and something popped up—just a bunch of symbols and letters in no particular order that went on for pages and pages. I took it out and put the other disc in. Same thing. There was something on the discs but I assumed my computer wasn't compatible with them. I looked at the other DVDs I'd taken from Randy's. I went through *Gnomeo and Juliet,* and tried most of the Disney classics. All the movies played. I held the two mystery discs in my hand, thinking. I needed someone who was computer savvy enough to figure out how to make them play. And she lived right next door. Tonja.

Chapter 36

I hadn't wanted to involve Tonja in anything to do with Randy but I needed help. She knew all about computers and best of all was in very close proximity. I decided to call her. I looked at the clock. It was only nine thirty and hopefully she was still up. She answered on the first ring.

"Hey Tonja, it's Alex."

"Oh, hi Alex! How are you? I'm so happy to hear from you. I was afraid . . ."

"No, no, no. It's all good."

"Really? I just want you to know I haven't been back to that club. I kind of realized it's not my thing, after all."

"Oh, okay. Well . . . it's your life. So whatever you need to do. Hey listen. I'm sorry to bother you this late but I have a couple of discs that my computer is having trouble reading. Do you know what I should do?"

"I'll come right over." She started to hang up.

"No wait! Can't you just tell me on the phone? I hate to bother you."

"No bother. I'll be right there." *Click.*

Two minutes later I heard a knock at my door. I opened it to Tonja.

"Hi, Alex!" She gave me a big hug. "Sarah's sleeping?"

"Yeah. Thanks so much for coming over. Do you want something to drink?"

"No." She spotted my computer on the bar and headed over to it. "Let me take a look." She popped the disc in and hit a couple of keys.

"Oh, I get it. You just need to download this software." She hit an icon on my desktop and something started downloading. Once that was done. She hit another couple of keys and put the disc in again. This time when it started to play you could clearly see what it was. A list of business files. I quickly hit the eject key and took the disc out.

"What was all that?" she asked.

"Just some of my business stuff. I couldn't get it to open."

"Really? Where are the other discs? You said you had a few you couldn't open?"

"Right. I think I can handle it. Thanks so much."

"Are you sure? I'm here. And maybe the other discs will need different applications."

"I've bothered you too much all ready. I've got it under control. Thanks again."

I hurried her out the door, thanking her profusely, and headed back to my computer. I picked up the phone and started to call Jakes, then thought better of it. How was our "break" going to affect solving this case? I decided to wait and see if there was anything interesting on the disc first.

I went to check on Sarah. Gratefully, she was still sound asleep. I pulled her blankets around her and kissed her forehead. I put on my most comfortable robe and got situated on the sofa with a cup of coffee, then put the disc back into the computer.

There were several files on it. I downloaded, then started opening them. Most had to do with business. It seemed Randy had a few things going for him, and given his history I had to wonder how many were illegal.

Some of the files were just filled with names and numbers. I assumed they were either partners or clients, along with the amount of money he'd gotten from them. What surprised me was that I recognized some of the names. In fact, I saw a couple of people whose money he had already stolen once before. How he ever got them to trust him again I'd never know. There were some well-known names, too. Celebrities, politicians . . . I'd need somebody with a business degree to translate a lot of this, but what I was interested in was The Trois ou Plus Club.

I kept opening and closing files, scrolling, and finally came to a page with a fleur-de-lis right at the top.

Bingo.

It was a 22-page document.

I went back to the top and started reading and, sure enough, this was the partnership agreement that spelled out the fact that Randy was part owner of the club.

Halfway through, I found the names of the partners, along with the percentage of ownership. Randy owned 30 per cent of the club, while four other men split the other 70 per cent. However, Randy was the largest single shareholder.

I didn't see the amount of each man's investment listed anywhere. Maybe there was a separate form for that.

I pulled a pad over and wrote down the names and addresses of the four partners.

I continued to look through other folders until I found another one connected to the club. It seemed to be a list of members, their real names along with phony names. There was "Patti Dennis," with "Vivica" next to it.

I sat back on the sofa. This was not good. For one thing we had four more suspects in the form of Randy's partners. And then, in the other file, we had a large list of suspects which were probably club members.

I took a second and looked out at the canal. My God! This was huge! With this information Jakes could possibly solve the case. I turned my attention back to the computer.

And then someone knocked at my door.

Chapter 37

It was after midnight. I had no idea who could be at my door at this hour. I looked out the front window and saw Harry's Toyota still parked out front. But no Harry. I peeked out the window and saw him standing on my porch. At least I thought it was Harry; he had his back to me. Wait a second. I had never seen Harry's face. What if something happened to him? What if this was the guy with the cowboy boots? I looked around, trying to find a weapon I could use. There was a poker by the fireplace. I ran over to get it as I heard another knock. This time it was louder. With the poker in hand, I got behind my front door and slowly pulled the curtain away from the window. The man was still there. Then I realized it couldn't be Harry. Harry was much shorter than this person. I started to panic as he turned to face me. Oh my God! It was Jakes! I opened the door and he stepped in.

"What are you do—"

Before I could finish my question he put his finger to his lips and mouthed, "Don't say anything." Closing the door behind us he pulled me into a long, deep kiss.

He broke away from me and still with his finger on his lips, led me across the room. Grabbing a blanket he put it around me, tugging me outside to the dock. After firmly shutting the door, he sat me down in a chair.

"Okay. Now we can talk," he said in a hushed tone.

"What the hell is going on?" I was pissed and confused.

"Shhhh. Keep your voice down. Someone has been following you, Alex. And I think your house is bugged, and your phone, too."

"What? Who?" I was incredulous.

"I'm not sure but I followed you after you left Randy's and someone was on your tail. I also think they were listening to your conversation with Wayne the night you went to Patti's. How else would someone know you were going there?"

This was a lot of information to take in and I was overwhelmed. And hurt.

"What's with the kiss? I thought you said you wanted a 'break?'"

"Are you nuts? I don't want a break. I said that for the benefit of who-ever was listening to our conversation."

"And what you said at the Farmer's Market?"

"Same thing. I wanted it to appear as if we were breaking up."

"Why didn't you just tell me?"

"I thought it would look more realistic if you didn't know."

Okay so I was relieved, but also a little insulted.

"I'm an actress, Jakes. That's my job." He shrugged. "Are you kidding me? Wait a second. Where's Harry?"

"Harry was never here. I've been out front the whole time. I want them to think you and I are over and that I had a friend look after you."

I couldn't do anything but stare at him. I had been on an emotional roller coaster because of this man and it was all just pretend? I had to hand it to him, though, he was good. I shook my head. Then I smacked him on the shoulder.

"Ow! That hurt."

"You deserve more than that after what you put me through!" I grabbed him and hugged him hard. "Oh my God!" I said pushing him away. "I told Sarah about Randy tonight."

"How did she take it?"

"She took it well, I mean I guess well. She cried a little and said that Randy and my Dad can keep each other company. That was sweet, huh?"

"Maybe the fact that Randy had been gone for most of her life took the sting out of it."

"No doubt. I know she still feels the loss, though." I looked around. "Are you sure we can talk out here?"

"Yes, I'm sure. What is it?"

"You're never going to believe what I found! I have some amazing information." I said.

"I have some, too. You go first."

"No, you. Yours can't be as amazing as mine. What did you find?"

"There were definitely no cops assigned to watch the Trois ou Plus Club, so there's some other way that Rockland knew you were there."

"What about what happened at Randy's house?"

"That actually was a nine-one-one call. There's a record. It was a woman's voice that called it in. Now you."

"It's crazy! You're not going to believe it. Sarah and I wanted to watch a movie tonight. We put in the DVDs that I took from Randy's. Two wouldn't play."

"Okaaay. That's very interesting, Alex, but—"

"That's not the news, you dope," I said, cutting him off. "Sarah fell asleep so I put one in my computer and with a little help from Tonja . . ."

"Tonja? What does she have to do with this?"

"Nothing! Everything. I mean she's a computer programmer and the disc wouldn't play at first so I called her and she came over and downloaded some software and then it played! And guess what? It's all Randy's business files!"

"What? How did they end up in those DVD boxes?"

"I have no idea. Obviously he didn't want anyone to find them and thought that would be a good hiding place."

"I guess it would have been. If you hadn't gone over there to get Sarah's stuff they probably would have been thrown out."

"Listen to what I found. It really makes the list of suspects a lot longer . . ."

He listened intently, interrupting only a couple of times to ask for clarification.

"Your ex-husband must have been a helluva con man," he said, when I was done.

"Yeah, well, he conned me."

"You're right about the suspect pool," Jakes said. "It's just increased by leaps and bounds."

"What do we do?" I asked. "Turn it over to Rockland?"

"That would probably be the right thing to do," Jakes admitted. "Probably the best thing to do for you and Sarah."

"But what about you?" I asked. "What's good for you? How do we get you reinstated?"

"Like I said, it feels personal. If I could solve this case, I'd get reinstated," Jakes said. "Of course, it'd be even better if Rockland ended up lookin' like a chump."

"Well," I said, "if we solve this we'll all get what we want. So what do we do, Jakes? Question all these suspects?"

"Too many people and too little time. That'd take forever," he said, "The smart thing to do is pare down the suspect pool." He was quiet for a moment. "So, what did you find on the other disc?" Jakes asked.

I couldn't believe it.

"Alex, what's wrong?"

"I haven't looked at them yet. I was so caught up in the first DVD I never even thought of the other one! Whatever's on it can't be as good as what was on the first one."

Really?

Chapter 38

We quietly closed the French doors behind us. Jakes held his finger to his lips and gestured to the phone. He went over to it and picked up the receiver. He opened up the back of the phone and pointed to a little tiny disc and nodded. I guess that meant he had found a bug. He put the phone back together and walked around the living room looking in the lamps and under the tables. He pointed to one that was next to the sofa by the fireplace and nodded again. I just shook my head in disbelief. Why would someone want to bug my home? What did they think I knew? It was very creepy. I went over to the coffee pot and gestured I would make more. He nodded and grabbed a notepad and pen from the kitchen drawer.

I'll put the other disc in. Where is it? he quickly wrote.

I pointed to the counter.

He grabbed it and pushed it into my computer.

I wanted to check on Sarah so I pointed down the hall and then put one finger in the air gesturing that I'd be back in a minute.

She was still fast asleep. I double checked the windows and pulled her blankets up again. On my way back to the living room I stopped in the bathroom to splash my face with water and look at my tired self in the mirror. This whole case was getting out of control. Who had bugged my house? And why? How had they gotten in without me knowing? I checked the window in the bathroom, turned off the light and headed down the hall to the living room.

The computer was facing Jakes and he was facing me, so I couldn't see what he was seeing on the screen. He held a coffee mug in one hand, poised halfway between the top of the table and his mouth. Frozen there. His mouth was open and he was kind of squinting at the screen. I ran behind him to take a look and had to cover my mouth so I wouldn't scream.

It was a movie, of sorts. Taken on someone's cell phone from the looks of it. It was dark and the focus was in and out but I could definitely tell where they were. It was The Director's Room at Trois ou Plus. And it was obvious what was going on. Sex! A group of people all engaged in some form of sexual activity. It was so blurry I couldn't exactly make out what was happening but got the general idea. The sound was muffled; I could hear people laughing. Jakes quickly hit the sound icon on my computer and brought the volume down. Then the picture went dark, as if the person holding the cell phone had put it in a pocket. The video kept playing. It was pulled back out and panned around the room. And that's when I saw them. Randy was leaning against a back wall holding a drink, wearing a cop's uniform, laughing. And right next to him, also wearing a uniform and laughing, was Sam Rockland!

Jakes and I looked at each other. Now both our mouths were open. And then we looked back to the screen. It was hard to believe what we were seeing but clearly undeniable. Randy and Rockland knew each other. Well. Jakes paused the video and grabbed my hand.

He quietly opened the door to the patio and brought me outside. He closed the door behind us.

"What the hell?" I said. "What is happening? That disc . . ."

"I know. It's pretty clear that Rockland and Randy knew each other, probably met at that club," Jakes said. "They looked pretty chummy."

"Wait a minute," I said. "Randy owned a piece of the club. You don't think Rockland owns—"

"I don't know," he said, following my train of thought, "but I'd love it if that was the case. If Rockland's also a part owner it makes him a suspect."

"And what about the bugs in my house? Who put them there?"

"Rockland, possibly. On the other hand anybody can buy bugging equipment and plant them."

"So do you think Rockland was having me followed?"

"Probably. I didn't get a good look at the guy, and then I lost him in traffic."

"But why? Why bug me?"

"Maybe he wants to know what you and I know."

I took a moment to process this.

"Do you think he could have killed Randy?"

"Could be. But that's quite a stretch." He shook his head as if trying to make sense of it. "Let's watch some more."

We went back into the house and I got my headphones out of the kitchen drawer. I plugged them into the computer and un-paused the video.

I studied the other people in the room and didn't recognize anyone else. Then the camera quickly scanned around the room and towards the floor. For a brief second I could see someone's shoes. The shoes of whoever was taking the video. They were cowboy boots with turquoise tips. Then it abruptly ended. I wildly pointed to the screen. This time I grabbed Jakes' hand and pulled him outside.

"Those are the boots I saw on Mulholland and at Randy's!" I said.

"Are you sure?"

"I'm sure." We went back inside and played that section again. I was positive they were the same cowboy boots I'd seen before.

"You're sure?" he mouthed. I nodded and we continued watching.

It looked like a new video, taken at Trois ou Plus as well. I could see the dais and the mattresses on the floor in the Director's Room—minus any people. It looked like somebody wanted to take a tour of the club. Each theme room was shot and the hallway, too. As he traveled down the hall, he ended up in front of a nondescript door. I could hear voices coming from inside. The door was pushed open and I recognized that it was the same office I had been to with George. Suddenly the picture was sideways and down, as if the cameraman was trying to hide the fact that he had a cell phone and was recording. Then it went black, like it was shoved into a pocket but I could still hear voices. One was clearly Rockland. He was speaking to someone. I recognized the other voice. It was Randy's. The cell phone was slowly pulled out again and panned across the room. Rockland was sitting behind the desk and Randy was sitting across from him on the sofa next to the bookcase. I could even see the little clay figure that Sarah had made for him. It looked like this was their office—Randy's and Rockland's. I pushed the volume up but couldn't make out what they were saying. I shook my head and handed the headphones to Jakes. He put them on, listened for a second and shook his head. He grabbed my hand again and we went outside.

Chapter 39

It had started raining again so we took the blanket and draped it over both our heads. It was like our own version of the cone of silence from "Get Smart".

"What does this all mean?" I had a pretty good idea but I wanted to hear it from him.

"It means Rockland bugged your house."

"How can you be so sure? Couldn't it be the guy with the boots?"

"Either or. They're probably working together. I'm going to remove the one from your lamp. I'll make it seem like it shorted out. Let's leave the one on your phone so it doesn't look suspicious. Just remember not to say anything when you use it that would give away what you know. Okay?"

He opened the door and walked into the house, with me following. He dropped the wet blanket on the floor and headed for the lamp by the fireplace. Poking his head under the shade he pulled out a little disc. He carried it to the kitchen sink, filled a glass halfway with water and then dropped the disc in. I couldn't imagine what that must have sounded like on the other end. I gathered up the two Randy discs, returning them back to their "movie" cases and put them in with Sarah's other DVDs.

Jakes quickly made a second sweep of the house. Finding no other bugs he said, "I've gotta go back to the club."

"Back to the club?" I asked. "Why?"

"If that's Rockland's office—Rockland's and Randy's—then maybe there's something in there that'll point to them being in business together. I want to have a look around."

"There is something."

"How can you be so sure?"

"Because I saw it when I was nosing around the office. The night I was at the club."

"What was it?"

"I'm not one hundred percent sure, but it looked like a purchase agreement." Before Jakes could ask me why I wasn't sure, I went on. "I got interrupted when I was looking at it. George knocked on the door warning me that someone was coming. One of the club employees made us leave."

"I've got to find it."

"Well then, I'm going with you."

"No," he said. "If I get caught in there, I'm in trouble. If you're with me, you're in trouble, too."

"I've already been to the club," I said. "I'll be able to take us right to the office and the file. You'll have to . . . stumble around until you find it. You need me so you can be in and out faster."

"You might be right."

"You know I'm right," I said. "We're in this together from now on, remember?"

"Okay," he said, "okay, so we'll go in together."

"When?"

He looked at his watch. "Two hours."

"Tonight?"

"We have to go in while they're closed," he said. "We should leave here at three a.m."

"Sarah. I can't."

"Oh, right. It's too late to ask Tonja to watch her . . ."

"Definitely."

"So tonight's off," he decided. "I'll find out when they close, when the cleaning crew comes in and leaves, and when they open."

"Can we go in tomorrow night?"

"You've got a lot of confidence in me."

"Yes, I do." I didn't even bother stifling a yawn. "I'm too old for this middle of the night stuff. I'm pooped."

"Early call tomorrow?"

"No, thank goodness. Sarah to school then I'm in at 9. Are you leaving me or staying over?"

"I'm not leaving you. Not with Rockland on the loose."

"How are you going to handle him, anyway, with him being the detective in charge?"

"I'm going to investigate him."

"What kind of investigate?"

"The kind I.A. conducts when they think a cop's dirty," he said. "I'm gonna look at his record inside and out."

"Hoping to find that he owns a side business?" I asked. "Like a swingers club?"

"Maybe, but that wouldn't be enough," he said. "I have to find some sort of connection between him and blue boots."

"They were actually turquoise." I said. "What kind of a connection do you think they have?"

"You saw how he kept putting his phone in his pocket, and then taking it out?" Jakes said. "My bet is he was gathering material for blackmail."

"To blackmail Randy? Or Rockland?"

He shrugged. "Maybe both."

"So then turquoise boots can't be a suspect for Randy's killing. I mean, why kill him if he was blackmailing him?"

"Something might've gone wrong. Anyway, I'll find out." He pulled me to him and kissed me. I tried to pull away but he started working his way down my neck. Unbuttoning my pajamas he was making my knees weak, but I finally—gently—pushed him away.

"Right now? It's two in the morning."

"No time like the present." He turned off the lights and led me into my bedroom.

"Aren't you kind of tired?" I whispered behind him. I hated sounding like a fuddy duddy, but c'mon! I had to be up in the morning. He ignored me as he closed the door and unbuttoned his jeans peeling them off.

I gave him the once over. He looked damn good. He laid back on my bed, naked but for a smile. I couldn't help but smile back.

"Oh what the hell," I said. "I'll sleep when I'm dead."

I pulled off my pajama pants and jumped on top of him.

Chapter 40

American Popstar was still using a lot of our parking spaces but I managed to find one out by the back forty, meaning far away from the Artist's Entrance. Good news, though, I had listened to the radio on the drive in and they said no rain for most of the day. But a storm was supposed to be rolling in later tonight.

As I was walking across the lot I saw a car leaving and swore it was Patti driving. I opened my mouth to yell, but it was no use. She never would have heard me. I flapped my arms trying to get the guard's attention to stop her but he just looked at me like I was a crazy person. She pulled out and made a left. I strained to see through the cars and the fence, and was sure it was Patti.

Damn!

From the looks of Patti's house the night George and I were there, I thought she had left town for good. What was she doing at the studio? And how did she get in? Once she had resigned, her pass would have been taken away. She would have had to be somebody's guest, and her name would be left at the gate.

I moseyed over to the guardhouse. Dammit! The guard was new so it could be more difficult to get information from him. I put on my most charming smile and gave it a go.

"Hi there! I'm Alexis Peterson." I put out my hand.

"Oh, hello, Miss Peterson. I know who you are," he said, shaking my hand.

"You're new here, right? I wanted to introduce myself."

"That's nice of you. Yeah, I just started last week."

"Well, welcome!" I turned as if I was going into the building and then looked back. "By the way, I think I just saw my ex make-up artist leaving the studio. Was that Patti Dennis I just saw driving away?" I asked.

He looked at his clipboard. "Why, yes, it was."

"That's funny, I thought she quit."

"She had a pass waiting for her," he said. "She was somebody's guest."

"I wonder whose?" I said, innocently.

He smiled and said, "Lemme check." He looked it up and said, "She was here to see Kathy Grant."

Kathy. Our body make-up person. And Patti's close friend.

"I'm sorry I missed her," I said. "Oh, well. Welcome again! I'll be seeing you every morning!"

"Thanks, Ma'am."

I hated "Ma'am" but I let it go. I couldn't wait to get inside and find Kathy. I dropped my stuff off in my dressing room. As I was pulling my script out of my bag, there was a knock at my door. I opened it to find Marcus.

"Hey, Alex. How are you? I thought we should run the new scenes." That stopped me cold.

"What new scenes?" I asked fearfully.

"The scenes that we got last night. The show is short."

Oh no. I'd been so distracted with the DVDs I'd found I never checked my email the night before.

"Marcus, I never got them!" I looked around my room and there on my coffee table was a packet. I pulled out the pages. Three new scenes I'd yet to look at. Let alone memorize!

"Give me a few minutes to check them out and I'll come find you."

I hustled him out of my room and read the pages. Nothing too difficult. They had added a love scene between Felicia and Brandon. Uh oh. And a one-page monologue for me at the very end. Crap. I quickly put on my love scene uniform of men's boxers and a tube top then sat down to concentrate on my lines. Thank God I'm a quick study! I mean literally thank GOD. I swear I have a good memory from having to memorize catechism when I was a kid in Catholic School. It doesn't take me too long to get dialogue in my head and it sure does come in handy on days like today.

Then I realized I was going to need body make-up. Perfect. I'd call Kathy and ask her to come to my room to do it and then grill her about Patti. I picked up the phone; Kathy answered on the first ring.

"Make-up. Kathy speaking."

"Hey Kathy, it's Alex. How are you?"

"Hi, Alex. Fine. You want to speak with George?"

"No. Not George. You. Would you mind coming down to my room to do body makeup? I have three added scenes I didn't know about and I'm going kind of crazy."

"Uhhh . . ."

"Please? Just today." I knew as a rule make-up and hair didn't like to do actors and actresses in their dressing rooms, unless it was an emergency.

"Okay. I'll be down in five minutes." She said reluctantly as she hung up the phone.

I looked over my lines again and remembered I was supposed to find Marcus. I plopped down on my sofa and called his room, telling him to come to my room in ten minutes. Then there was a very light knock on my door.

"Come in!" I shouted. Kathy popped her head in. "Hi there! Come on in. Thanks so much for doing this. Crazy day!"

"Sure, no problem." She sounded like it was a problem, though. She put her make-up kit on the counter and pulled out a wet sponge. "Spread your legs, please."

I assumed the position. Hands on hips and parted legs.

"Whoa! That's cold! Never quite get used to it."

Kathy proceeded to work in silence. While I proceeded to grill her.

"So that was crazy, huh? Patti being here? How is she anyway?" Kathy was a sphinx. I pressed on. "She was here this morning. You left her a pass?"

"Oh. Yeah." She took the sponge and wiped it over the back of my thigh.

"Aghhh! Cold!"

"Sorry." Not.

I turned to face her and taking the sponge out of her hand I looked her straight in the eye and asked, "Where is she, Kathy?"

"I can't tell you."

"Did she come here to borrow money? Or your car? Or maybe you gave her your apartment key?"

When her head snapped up I knew I'd hit it. I thought Patti had ditched us at the club and left town, but she had apparently needed a place to hide out.

"Come on, Kathy," I said. "You know Patti's in trouble. She could get you in trouble, too. Are you letting her stay at your place?"

She looked down. "I asked her what was going on, why she needed a place to hide out. I mean, why had she quit so suddenly, what was she running from?"

"What did she tell you?"

"Some BS story about an old boyfriend stalking her and that she needed a place to hide."

"Did she tell you that was why she quit her job, too?"

"Well . . . yeah."

"You think Patti's the type to let some creepy ex-boyfriend make her quit her job and hide out?"

"No, I didn't think so, and then she said something else kind of weird."

"What?" Kathy hesitated so I repeated the question only stronger this time. "What? It's important, Kathy."

"She said, 'they found me'. When I asked her what that meant she just shook her head. She looked really scared."

"She's in trouble, Kathy, but it's not a stalker she's hiding from. It's a killer."

"A . . . what?"

"She knows something about who killed my ex-husband, Randy," I said. "She needs to be found by the police before the killer finds her. She needs to help us—the police catch the killer."

"OmiGod!"

"If she's at your place, and you go home," I said, "you could be in danger, you know."

"Me? I didn't do anything—I don't know any—"

"The killer doesn't know that," I said. "Look, you know I'm dating a police detective, right?"

"Y-yes."

"Well, tell me the truth and I'll have him take care of it. I swear, you'll be safe."

She thought about that.

"You won't be betraying Patti, Kathy," I said, softly, "you'll be helping her."

"She's—she's not at my place. She's at my folks' townhouse. They're in Europe. I—I gave her the key. She said it would only be for a day or two."

"Tell me the address, Kathy," I said. "I'll make sure nothing happens to her, or you."

"Are—are you sure she won't be mad?" Kathy asked.

"She might be mad," I said, "but maybe she won't be dead."

Haltingly, she gave it to me. It was in the flats of Beverly Hills, bordering Century City.

Chapter 41

While throwing my street clothes back on, I called Herbie and told him I had a family emergency. It wasn't a total lie. Patti wasn't family but this WAS an emergency.

In my car, once I cleared the parking lot, I Blue-toothed Jakes.

"Alex?" his voice came over the speaker. "What's going on?"

"I saw Patti leaving the studio this morning," I said, "I tried but I couldn't stop her. Turns out she was here to see Kathy, in make-up. They're friends."

"And?"

"She's got the keys to Kathy's parents' townhouse. She told Kathy she needed to hide out for a couple of days. That 'they had found her'."

"They? Did she say who they were?"

"Not that Kathy said. It can't be good though."

"You're right."

"I have the address and I'm on my way over there."

"Give it to me," he said. "I'll meet you. And Alex?"

"Yeah?"

"Stay in your car. Don't do a thing until I get there!"

I pulled onto the street where Kathy's parents had their townhouse. When I spotted the numbers I slowed down. I parked a few doors down and settled in to wait for Jakes. The townhouse was brick, with a staircase up to the front door.

I was only there a few minutes when I noticed a man walking toward the townhouse. I tried to get a look at his face but he kept his head down, only looking around from time to time. I hadn't seen a car pull up so I had no idea where he had come from. He could be a salesmen—or Jehovah's Witness—I guess but something about him made my antennae go up. He looked strangely familiar. My heart caught in my throat. He looked like the guy that approached me on Mulholland, at least in stature and hair color. As he started running up the brick stairs I looked closely at his shoes. I couldn't tell from where I was if he was wearing cowboy boots or not, but the tips did seem blue.

As I watched, he reached the door and looked around. I laid down on the seat of my car just in case he caught sight of me. I was afraid to raise my head but slowly I peeked out from behind my dashboard. He was no-where to be seen. I wasn't sure if he had left or if Patti let him in. Or, God forbid, if he had forced himself in. I didn't know what to do. Where the hell was Jakes?

It was only a few seconds later when the guy came out, dragging Patti with him. She was not really resisting, but clearly looked terrified. I start-ed dialing Jakes when I saw her suddenly trying to yank her arm from his grasp. She grabbed the wrought iron banister at one point, halfway down the stairs, and he tried pulling her free. When he couldn't he hit her, and that's when I dropped my phone and jumped out of my car.

I didn't do it consciously. If I had, maybe I would have gone into my trunk for a tire iron or something. No, even when I thought about it later I didn't remember opening the door and getting out. All of a sudden I was just on the street, running towards them.

"Hey! Hey!" I yelled. "Leave her alone!"

They both looked over at me and then Patti yelled, "Alex!"

They froze for a moment, and then he started trying to pull her again. She held on for dear life. I reached the bottom of the stairs and looked up. Our eyes met and he knew I recognized him. It was definitely the guy I had seen that night on Mulholland. He was a big man, bigger than I even remembered. But there was no question about who he was. There was no cowboy hat, but he had on those turquoise-tipped boots.

"Let her go, damn it!" I said, and started up the stairs. Now, I did re-member doing that later, but I couldn't have said why.

Patti was holding the banister with one hand and beating on him with the other. When I reached them I was confused as to what to do. I'd never punched anyone in my life. Except when I was acting. At first I grabbed his arm and tried to pull him off her. He was too strong. When that didn't work I punched him, first on the arm a few times, and then I hit him on the head. All that did was hurt my hand. Like I said, he was a big man.

He had a look of complete indifference as he swatted at me with one arm, knocking me back. It was as if he didn't consider me a danger, at all. And that pissed me off. I summoned up my inner Ninja and lacing my fingers together, formed a club with my hands. I hit him as hard as I could on his back, just below his neck. That got his attention.

"You little bitch. I'm gonna take care of you once and for all." He spat at me, as he turned to face me. And I do mean spat.

I wiped my face off as I backed away from him. He was reaching for me, forgetting Patti for the moment. I grabbed for the other banister as I felt my heel slip on the edge of a step.

Then I was falling.

I landed at the bottom of the stairs. As I watched, he stopped trying to pull her from the banister. He looked at me and for a moment I thought he was going to come after me. Then he took something from his pocket, and jabbed Patti with it. Abruptly she released her hold and grabbed her stomach.

He had stabbed her, and now he was coming down the stairs towards me.

Chapter 42

He ran down the stairs at me, the bloody knife poised in mid air. I put my arms up in front of my body thinking he was going to stab me like he did Patti. Just then I heard a voice cry out.

"You leave those girls alone you big bully!"

He turned toward who was yelling at him then looked back at me. I thought I was going to be next. He surprised the hell out of me when he leaped over me. I wanted to turn to see where he'd gone, but right behind him, Patti was tumbling down the stairs. Before I knew it she was on me and we were tangled on the sidewalk.

I heard a car starting down the block and then pulling away from the curb. I untangled myself from Patti and then rolled her over to see if she was alive. She was, her face etched in pain. She was wearing a white blouse, now soaked with blood.

Another car screeched to the curb and Jakes jumped out.

"Alex, damn it—"

"Patti's been stabbed! Call nine-one-one!" I shouted. "It was him! The guy from Mulholland. I recognized him. He just drove off."

"Take your jacket off and put pressure on her stomach!" I could hear him telling the emergency operators the address where we were as he jumped back into his car and pulled away.

I quickly pulled off my jacket and pressed it to her wound, trying to stop the bleeding. She was losing consciousness.

"You're going to be okay, Patti." I stroked her forehead, trying to re-assure her. Her eyes fluttered a few times and then she passed out. "Oh, God! Please be all right." I whispered to myself.

Jakes got back to us just as the ambulance arrived.

"I couldn't find him," he said, crouching over us.

"Are you all right?"

"I'm okay," I said. "Patti passed out."

"Keep pressure on that . . ." he said.

We tried to staunch the flow of blood. We kept talking to her hoping maybe she'd come to, but she was out cold. When the ambulance came they quickly put her in the back. I jumped in with her. I felt like it was the least I could do. After all, I was indirectly responsible for what had happened.

"Alex?" Patti said, reaching her hand out, struggling to come to. Her voice was muffled by the oxygen mask on her face.

I looked at the attendant, and he nodded, so I moved next to her and took her hand. She held my hand tightly all the way to the hospital. I leaned over her, telling her she was going to be all right.

When we got to Cedar Sinai Hospital, attendants hurriedly wheeled her into the emergency room. Jakes was there ahead of us, and he made a doctor come look at me.

"I'm fine," I said.

"You're bleeding, Alex," Jakes said.

"I am?" I looked down, saw that my sleeve was torn and red with blood. Also, my knees had been skinned. I weakly looked at Jakes and said, "You should have seen the other guy."

A nurse took me into an examining room. And then in walked an incredibly gorgeous man. Apparently this was my doctor. And apparently I was going to be okay if I was noticing his good looks.

"Hi, Alexis. I'm Dr. Hart. What happened here?" he asked as he checked out my skinned knees.

"Oh, no biggie. I fell down a couple of stairs."

"Really? Fell down some stairs, huh." He pushed my bangs aside. "What about here. Does this hurt?" He asked touching my forehead."

"Not much, no. I'm okay."

"Wow, you're a tough one, aren't you?" He smiled and showed off dazzling white teeth. This guy should be on television I thought to myself, not wasting his time saving human lives.

He cleaned up my scrapes and wiped my forehead with antiseptic. When I was bandaged he said, "Sit here for a little while."

"How's Patti?" I asked. "The woman I came in with?"

"I'll check for you," he said, "but I want you to sit here for a minute or two. It looks like you may have hit your head when you fell, so stay put. I don't want you keeling over."

"Okay."

As he left, Jakes came in.

"How's Patti?" I asked him.

"They're working on her," he said, taking my hand. "How are you?"

"I'm fine." I was sitting up on an examination table, my legs dangling, bandages on my knees and elbow. I had a bump on my head right at my hairline, but I hadn't been cut there.

"Alex," he asked, "what happened?"

"What happened is I almost got Patti killed."

"Start from the beginning . . ."

So I did, from the moment I had pulled up to the curb in my car . . .

". . . maybe," I finished, "if I hadn't run to be a hero and got myself involved, he wouldn't have stabbed her."

"That's not so," he said. "He was probably taking Patti someplace to kill her. If you hadn't intervened, he could have driven off with her and killed her at his leisure. You probably saved her life, Alex."

"If she survives," I said. "Where's that doctor? He said he'd check on her for me."

"I'll check," he said. "You stay here."

"Alright."

"I mean it, Alex," he said.

"I know."

He went to the door, but didn't go out. He backed up and turned to me.

"There are some uniforms here," he said. "The hospital must have called them because of the knife wound."

"Should we try to get out?"

"No," he said. "If Patti survives, she's gonna mention you."

"What about you?"

"We'll see," he said, "but she'll definitely tell them about you, so just tell them you went there to see her, and saw them struggling. Tell the truth from there."

"Are they going to call Rockland?"

"Probably," he said.

"How do I deal with that? He could be Randy's killer."

"Just stay calm. Tell the cops that you and Patti work together and she quit suddenly. You decided to check on her and walked into this situation. If Rockland shows up, tell him the same thing."

"What about you? You should get out of here."

"No," he said, "we'll just tell them that you called me when you got here. We're a couple. That would be natural."

"Okay."

"Now relax, get your breath back. The key is to stick as close to the truth as possible."

"Right."

"And Alex?"

"Yeah?"

"Did the guy that attacked you know you recognized him?"

"Definitely. He said he was going to take care of me once and for all. Before that lady yelled out."

"What lady? You never mentioned a lady."

"She saved my life, Jakes. The guy was about to stab me when she yelled out for him to stop." He nodded and looked at the floor.

"Where was she when this happened?"

"I'm not sure. I had a lot going on at the time, ya know?"

"I'm gonna want to find her and talk to her. Don't mention this to the cops, okay? And for now you stay put. Understand?" He held me by my shoulders and kissed me someplace it didn't hurt, adding, "I'll check on Patti and come right back."

As he went out the door I briefly considered jumping down from the table and running out. Although I realized I wouldn't get too far with a hospital full of cops. At least I wouldn't have to concentrate on staying as close to the truth as possible if I got out of there. But I wanted to know how Patti was.

While I was weighing my options two uniformed policemen walked into the room.

Chapter 43

I had to show them identification and answer questions, just as Jakes had said. They wanted to know what happened, what I was doing there, if I knew the victim and the assailant. I told them that I worked with Patti and was concerned when she had suddenly quit our show. That I had heard she was staying at a mutual friend's house and decided to check on her because I was worried. I had driven up to find her being attacked by the assailant, whom I had never seen before. That part I lied about. And I left out the part of the neighbor who heroically saved my life.

They wrote it all down, and then told me I was going to have to talk to a detective. I hoped they weren't referring to Rockland. It was going to be tricky hiding what I knew about him and Randy, and that he had most likely bugged my home and phone. And even may have been behind Patti's stabbing.

They left, and Dr. Hart came back in, closing the door behind him.

"How's Patti?"

"She's still in surgery. So far she's stable." He said. "The knife did a bit of internal damage. Good going with keeping the pressure on her wound. Because of that her blood loss wasn't as extensive as it could have been."

"When will she be out?"

"An hour or so," he said "and then she'll be moved to recovery."

"When can I leave?" I asked. "I've got to pick up my kid from school in a few hours."

"How do you feel?"

"Fine."

"No dizziness?"

"None."

"Stand up."

I dropped down from the table and as soon as my feet hit the floor I swayed—or the room did. The doctor took my arm and steadied me.

"Sit back down," he said. "Can you have someone else pick up your child?" Dr. Hart whipped out his little tiny flashlight and pointed it in my eyes. "Let me take another look."

"Is there something wrong with me?"

"Nothing serious. But you were shaken up. It would be better if you didn't drive today."

The door opened suddenly and Detective Rockland strode in. "How is she, Doctor?" He was looking straight at me when he asked the question.

"Not seriously injured," the doctor said, "but she could use some rest."

"I can question her, then?" His gaze never left me.

The doctor straightened up and looked at Rockland. "For a few minutes," he said, "and then I want her to rest. Understand?"

"I understand."

My handsome doctor was a youngish man, and Rockland was imposing. I admired the way he stood up to him. I heart Dr. Hart.

"Call me if you need me," the doctor said to me.

"Thank you." I was close to begging him to stay with me but I thought better of it.

He left and Rockland moved closer, which I didn't appreciate.

"Could you back up please?" I asked, putting my hand out. "You're making me feel nauseous."

He backed up two steps. I wondered if he had seen Jakes in the hospital.

"You want to tell me what you were doin'?" he asked.

"I was going to see Patti," I said. "When I got there I saw her being assaulted, so I tried to help."

"How'd you know she was there?"

"She called me at the studio, said she wanted to talk," I lied, keeping Kathy out of it.

"About what?"

"She didn't say on the phone, but I had the feeling it was about Randy's murder."

Rockland hesitated, passed his hand over his mouth. He was looking right through me. I have to admit it was a little frightening. I had no idea what this man was capable of doing. Well actually I did. And that's what was scary.

"Who was the guy?"

"What guy?"

"The guy who stabbed your friend. The guy who knocked you around, Alex. Remember him?"

"I don't know."

"You never saw him before?" His look was penetrating.

I hesitated and took a breath. Hopefully he wouldn't notice how nervous I actually was.

"No," I said, "I've never seen him before."

"What about his car. Did he have a car?"

"I never saw one. It all happened very quickly, you know?" He stepped a little closer to me. "Please. Back. Up. I'm not feeling well. I'd hate to barf all over your nice suit." I smiled weakly.

He looked like he wanted to punch me, but instead he slowly took a step back. "So that's it?"

"That's it," I said. He stood there sizing me up. I got the feeling he didn't believe a word I was saying. "Why aren't you asking Patti these questions?"

"I was waiting for her to regain consciousness so I could," he said, "but she crashed and they kicked me out."

"What? Is she all right?"

"I don't know," he said, unconcerned. "I came over here to question you."

"She crashed and you didn't wait to see if she was okay?" I asked.

He shrugged. "I have a job to do."

"You're a sonofabitch, do you know that?" It was out of my mouth before I could stop it. "A first class SOB."

"You might be surprised to find out you're not the first person to call me that." He smiled.

I stood up, fought off a wave of dizziness and pushed past him, grabbing my purse.

"I'll be in touch, Miss Peterson," he called after me.

I wondered at the time what he would have done if I'd told him about the man from Mulholland?

Chapter 44

I hurried down the hall and went into the ladies room. I pulled out my cell phone and called Tonja. She picked up on the first ring.

"Hi Alex! How are you?"

"I'm okay. Well not really. I, uh, have a problem at work. I'm not going to be done in time to pick up Sarah from school."

"Say no more! I'll get her and take her to my house. Don't you worry about a thing."

"Thanks so much. I'll call and let you know what time I'll be back. Thanks, again. I really appreciate it."

"No problem, Alex. I'm happy to help."

She hung up and I looked in the mirror. Lord! I had a bruise that was coming up on my forehead; it was going to be a doozie. I quickly brushed my bangs over to hide it and headed back into the hall to find Patti. Unfortunately, I didn't know where she was. I didn't even know if she was on the same floor. I looked around and saw my doctor standing at a desk talking to a nurse.

"Doctor Hart!" I called. He turned and looked at me, said something to the nurse, then turned to face me as I approached him.

"Patti," I said. "What happened—is she—what happened to—"

"Calm down," he said. "She crashed, but she's all right. They took her to ICU."

"So she can't be questioned?"

"Not for a while," he said, "She's being closely monitored." He looked past me. I turned and over my shoulder saw Rockland just coming out of the examination room I'd been in. He had his cell phone in his hand, was in the act of closing it. He'd stayed behind to make a call.

To whom, I wondered?

"Do you know where my—Detective Jakes—the man I, my . . . my boyfriend is?"

"When they wheeled your friend to Intensive Care he went with her."

"And where is that?"

"One floor up."

"Thank you."

I hurried to the elevator, hoping Rockland wouldn't follow me.

I found Jakes standing outside of Intensive Care. There was no sign of Rockland behind me.

"I'm glad I found you," I said.

"Rockland?"

"Downstairs. He said Patti crashed so he came to talk to me. He didn't care if she'd made it or not. I was this close to smacking him. He's a real asshole."

"That he is. And then some. Thankfully, Patti's okay, but she can't talk."

"Has Rockland seen you yet?" I asked.

"No, but I think I'll go down and rattle his cage a little."

"I told him what happened, but I didn't tell him about recognizing the guy or the lady who yelled out."

"Okay, good to know," he said. "Look, wait for me here."

"Do you think it's smart to let him see you?"

"I want him off balance," Jakes said. "I want him to wonder what I know."

"What are you going to do?"

He held me by the arms, kissed me and said, "I'm gonna make him think I know more than I do. Wait here, I'll be right back."

I turned and looked through the window at Patti. With tubes running in and out of her and machines all around she looked very small and pale. I couldn't help but wonder if she was lying in there because of me, or if Jakes was right. She would have been dead if I hadn't gone charging in like the cavalry. Now she was just lying in a hospital bed, clinging to life by a thread. Either way it didn't seem I'd done her much good.

A nurse came out and I stopped her. "How is she?"

"It was close," the woman said, "but we're managed to stabilize her, again."

"Again?" I asked.

"Yes, we had her stable before she crashed."

"So it could happen again?"

"Oh, yes," she said. "It could." She touched my arm. "But maybe it won't."

Yeah, maybe, I thought, looking back at Patti.

Jakes later told me about his encounter with Rockland . . .

As the elevator doors opened Jakes prepared to step out, but Rockland was standing there.

"Up?" Jakes said.

"What are you doin' here?" Rockland demanded. "You have no right—"

"My girlfriend was assaulted," Jakes said. "I'm here to pick her up. She's upstairs, with her friend. You going up?"

"I was gonna check on the Dennis woman," Rockland said.

"She's all right," Jakes said. "Stable, but unconscious."

"So she can't talk?"

"She can't."

Rockland nodded, started to step away from the elevator. Jakes walked out.

"Of course," he said, "she could, but now she can't."

"What do you mean, she could?"

"She was lucid just for a few minutes," Jakes said. "She . . . talked."

"About what?"

Jakes shrugged. "She just . . . muttered some things about . . . blue boots? You know anything about that?"

"What? Blue Boots? No. She, uh, didn't say anything else?"

"Maybe a few things, but nothing that sounded important. I was just coming down to get some coffee. Alex and I'll stay around, in case she wakes up again."

Rockland stared at Jakes, then pointed his finger.

"If she identifies the guy who assaulted her you better let me know."

"Well sure, Sam," Jakes said. "Why wouldn't I?"

"Remember," Rockland said, "you're not carrying a badge, anymore."

"That's just temporary. I'll be back on duty soon."

"Well until then, stay out of my way."

Jakes spread his arms. "Am I in your way?"

"Just remember."

As Rockland started to walk away Jakes asked, "What about the Randy Moore murder? Any progress?"

Rockland pointed his finger at Jakes again and said, "Stay away from that case, and tell your girlfriend to stay away, too."

"Hey, you're the one who gave her access to his house."

"Yeah, and that was a mistake. Believe me, I won't make another one."

"Hey Sam," Jakes said, "we never plan to make mistakes . . . that's why they call them mistakes."

Rockland looked like he wanted to say something else, but in the end he just turned and walked away . . .

* * *

"I think I shook him with the comment about blue boots."

"What do you think he'll do?"

"Who knows?"

"What do you want him to do?"

Jakes didn't answer.

"Wait a minute," she said. "You want him to send turquoise boots after you, don't you?"

"No," he said, "not me, or you."

"You want him to send him after Patti," I said. "You think he'll do that here, in the hospital?"

Jakes looked around. We were still standing in front of Patti's room. "Let's find a lounge where we can talk," he said. "I found out some things I want to tell you about."

He took me by the elbow.

Chapter 45

We found a small lounge with a door we could close. There was a window, though, and we could still see down the hall towards Patti's room.

"What did you find out?"

"I called in some favors at headquarters," he said, "had somebody do an in-depth computer search for me."

"You gonna get into more trouble for that?"

"Could be, but it'll be worth it."

"What did you research?"

"Blue boots," he said. "Or, to be more exact, boots with turquoise tips. Do you know that when an arrest is made they put everything into the computer? And they've gone back years and done the same thing with old arrests."

I felt my eyes widen. "You found him," I said. "You found the guy with the turquoise boots."

"I did."

"Who is he?"

"His name is Vincent Carver," Jakes said. "He's got a long sheet, everything from stealing cars to assault."

"Has he been in jail?"

"No."

"Why not?"

"I think he's got a guardian angel."

I stared at him, then said, "Rockland?"

"That's my bet," Jakes said. "Rockland's name shows up on several reports as the arresting officer. As I said, Carver's never done time, and eventually the arrests stopped."

"So you think Rockland's been . . . what? Protecting him?"

"And maybe using him," Jakes said. "As a C.I., in the beginning, but maybe the relationship developed."

"A C.I.?"

"Confidential Informant," Jakes said. "Lots of cops have them. Criminals they protect in exchange for information."

"Oh," I said. "Um, do you have C.I.'s?"

"I've used them in the past, yeah," he said. "But I've never used one to kill people."

"So you think Rockland had Carver kill Randy, and try to kill Patti today?"

"Patti, yes," Jakes said. "I think that's obvious. But I can't prove a thing about Randy, yet. So far all we know is that they've been in the same room together."

"But with Carver taking secret pictures of them both," I said, "we're back to blackmail."

"Patti must know something," Jakes said. "That's why she was hiding, and that's why Carver tried to kill her."

"I have a question," I said.

"What is it?"

"Since I can identify the guy who attacked Patti as the same guy who was on Mulholland, doesn't that mean I'm a direct threat to Rockland? It does, right?"

He stared at me and said, "Yes, it does." He put his arm around me. "That's why you need to stay put. Do you understand? You're in danger. Big time."

"What should I do? Is Sarah safe?"

"She's at school now, right?"

"Yes. And I have Tonja getting her when she's out. She'll be at her house."

"Then she's fine. I'm thinking about what to do with you. I want to go back and find the neighbor who yelled out."

"What's the difference? I can identify Carver."

"Yeah, but maybe she can identify the car."

"You don't have an address for him from those arrest reports?"

"Outdated addresses, yes."

"Are you going to go and look for him?"

"I should," he said, "but I don't want to leave you alone. And I don't want to leave Patti unprotected."

"Well," I said, "I have a solution."

"And what's that?"

"Take me with you. I have to get my car from there, anyway."

"I could do that," he said, "but how does that solve the problem of Patti? Keeping her alive until she can talk."

"Are you sure Rockland will send Carver after her?" I asked.

"Rockland's a careful man. He wouldn't want anyone else to know what he was up to. I think Carver's the only one he'd use."

"Then we have to wait here for him to try."

"Unless we can catch him before he does," Jakes said. "If someone saw the license plate of the car—"

"What about Harry Slattery?" I asked. "You were going to use him to protect me. What about using him to protect Patti?"

He grabbed me by the shoulders and said, "You're a genius."

"I know that."

Chapter 46

Jakes made a call on his cell and Harry Slattery was in the hospital within half an hour.

"Harry, this is Alex."

"Ah," Slattery said, "I've heard a lot about you."

He shook my hand. For a big brute of a man he had a gentle hand-shake—or maybe it was just with me. He turned his black eyes toward Patti and his heavy black brows knitted. "That's her, huh?"

"That's her," Jakes said. "All you've got to do is help the doctors keep her alive. Understand?"

"Yeah, sure, Jakes," Slattery said. "You don't want me to let anybody in who might kill her. Am I lookin' for anybody in particular?"

"Yeah," Jakes said. "Fella named Vincent Carver."

"What's he look like?"

Jakes nodded to me.

"That's a face I'll never forget," I said. "Blondish, gray hair and light eyes. He's tall, kind of sad looking and he has a hawk nose. Oh and he always wears boots with turquoise tips."

"Turquoise?"

"Right."

"He the one who put her there?" Slattery asked, indicating Patti.

"That's right," Jakes said, "and he may come back to finish the job if I can't find him first."

"And what about Alex?" Slattery asked, "Is she gonna be here?"

"She'll be with me," Jakes said. "Keepin' her safe is my job. You've only got one thing to do."

"Keep that lady from gettin' killed," Slattery said.

"Right."

"Got it."

"You got your cell?" Jakes asked.

"Yeah, and your number's in it."

"Ditto," Jakes said. "Okay, I'll keep in touch."

"Don't worry about your friend," Slattery said to me. "I've got this."

I put my hand on his arm and said, "Thank you."

When he smiled the blackness of his beard made his teeth look so white.

Jakes grabbed my arm and said, "Come on."

As we drove he said, "Do you remember the general direction that the lady's voice came from?"

"If I had to guess I'd say within a house or two from the townhouse, but like I mentioned before I was kind of busy. Sorry, it's hard to say for sure."

"She had to be able to have seen you from inside her house. So it had to be fairly close."

"Unless she was walking a dog, or getting her mail, or something. But I don't remember seeing anybody on the street when I drove up." I turned to him. "Hey, wouldn't your department be doing this canvas already?"

"Somehow I don't think Rockland put in that call. He doesn't want anybody to find Carver."

Jakes parked in front of Kathy's parents' townhouse.

"This is a long block," I said. "It's going to take some time."

"Then we better get started."

I put my hand on his arm to keep him from getting out of the car. "Why don't we split up?"

"You're not a cop."

"Why do I have to be a cop to ask questions?" I said. "Besides, you don't have a badge to flash, either." He sighed. "You're right, but I don't want you to be alone."

"It's just a few houses. I'll have my cell with me."

He mulled this over for a few seconds.

"No. I don't want you going house to house alone. Besides it'll be faster if you're there for the woman to recognize you. If she saw you and Patti being attacked she might have seen his car, too. As for the other neighbors, we'll try to ask as few questions as possible. Do they know what happened? And did they see a car. If they did, then we'll ask for a description, or even a plate."

"And if they want to know why we're asking?"

"We'll just say we're with the department. We won't say which one. Let's go." And we got out of the car.

Jakes wanted us to start across the street, because somebody had to have been looking out their window. Anybody looking out the window on the same side of the block wouldn't have been able to see the front of the townhouse.

My man is so smart.

The neighborhood was an interesting blend of townhouses from the 1940's and the old Spanish white stucco, red-tile roofed houses that were built in the 1920's. There were also a few smaller houses built in the '50's.

We went to three separate townhouses first. The people we approached were all about 30 to 50 years old and not very willing to speak with us. They seemed wary about getting involved. From what I could tell, and Jakes concurred, they hadn't seen anything anyway.

The fourth person lived in an older, sort of rundown house circa 1950. He was a sweet older man of about 70 who recognized me. He invited us to come in for coffee. I signed an autograph for him and convinced him to answer our questions at the door. He was a fan, but he hadn't seen anything.

The fifth person lived in one of those cute Spanish bungalows. We walked under an archway heavy with blooming bougainvillea and onto a porch with two wicker rocking chairs and a small table. I rang the doorbell and an elderly woman cautiously peeked out the window of the front door. She took one look at me and her eyes got big. She put her wrinkled hands in front of her face and for a moment I thought she wasn't going to help. We heard some locks click and then she quickly opened the door. Before I knew what was happening she wrapped her thin arms around me and pulled me close to her. She was shaking and crying.

"Oh, you poor thing," she said.

Chapter 47

We both entered the woman's home. She looked to be about 75 years old and had gorgeous blue gray hair swept up in a French twist. Her skin was translucent and even though she had fine lines and wrinkles on her face and neck she was beautiful. She was so distraught I put my arms around her this time and held her.

"You're alright! I was so worried. How's the other girl?" she asked as she pulled out of our embrace.

"She's out of surgery and looks like she's going to be okay." I sort of told her the truth. I was hoping it was the truth, anyway. "I'm so grateful to you! You saved my life." Now we were both crying. "My name is Alexis Peterson and this is Frank Jakes."

"I'm Laureen Lester. Oh, thank goodness you're okay. I've been waiting for the police to come and question me about that horrible, horrible man. Please sit down and let me make us some tea. Or would you prefer coffee?"

I looked to Jakes.

"Coffee would be great, Ms. Lester—" Jakes started, but she cut him off.

"Oh, dear, just call me Lulu," she said. "All my friends do. Please. Sit down and make yourselves at home. I won't be but a minute. And she went off towards the kitchen.

Lulu Lester? It had a nice ring to it. Jakes and I looked around her home. It was beautifully furnished in the Deco Era. A gorgeous matching sofa and chair covered in what looked like authentic Maroon mohair with curved backs and arms and highly polished ornately carved dark wood trim. The walls were hung with beveled mirrors with bright cockatiels and tropical leaves in the center. There was a beautiful white baby grand piano in the corner of the room topped with framed black and white photos from the 30's and 40's. I walked over to look at them.

"Oh my God, Jakes. This is a photo of W.C. Fields. I think this is Lulu next to him." On closer inspection all the photos were of the greats from the silent era and beyond. Charlie Chaplin, Fred Astaire and Ginger Rogers. Even Bette Davis, Clark Gable and Joan Crawford. And there was Lulu next to all of them. "Who is she, do you think?" I asked Jakes.

"I was a dancer in my day." Lulu volunteered as she appeared in the doorway with a tray of coffee and cookies. "And those were my friends." She sat the tray down on the coffee table and joined us by the piano. "Those were the great days of Hollywood." She sighed. "Oh! The parties we had. What a time!"

I was fascinated. "Did you dance in the movies?"

"Oh my yes! I started on Broadway, you know. Then ended up moving to Hollywood in 1932. I was sixteen. I danced with Fred *before* there was a Ginger!"

"You were born in 1916? That means you're ninety-five years old?" I was incredulous. She looked amazing.

"Actually, I just turned ninety-six. But don't let it get around." She winked and smiled. "Come sit. It's so nice to have guests!"

We went over to the sofa and sat down as she poured us each coffee. "And what do you do for a living, dears?"

"I'm an actress. On *The Bare and the Brazen*. It's a soap opera."

"Oh, I dated an actor who was on a Soap Opera, back in the fifties for awhile. I believe it was called *Young Doctor Malone*. Ohhh! It was live in those days. Very hard work. If you can act on a soap, you can act any-where."

"You're right, Lulu," I said nodding and taking a bite of a delicious butter cookie. "I appreciate that."

"Thank you for being so brave. You really did save Alex's life," Jakes said.

"I'm not one of those nosey neighbors who's always prying into other people's lives, I want you to know. But I do like to keep abreast of what's going on around me. That's how you get to be ninety-six years old." She laughed.

"We're glad you do," Jakes said as he took my hand in his. Lulu no-ticed.

"Are you two a couple?"

"Yes, we are, Lulu," Jakes said, "and I want to find the man who put his hands on my girl."

Lulu leaned in close to Jakes and asked, "Are you gonna kick his ass?"

He leaned in also and said, "Just between you and me, Lulu, I'm gon-na do worse than that."

"Oh, good." Her eyes sparkled. "He deserves it."

"But I need to find him first," he said. "Can you help me with that?"

"Well," she said, sitting back, "I'm afraid I didn't see his face. I tried to, mind you but he kept looking down. I did notice that he had on unusual shoes. I'm blessed with perfect vision, even at my age. I could see those silly boots he was sporting. They had blue tips."

"And his car? Did you see that?"

"Oh yes," she said, "it was a beautiful Lincoln."

"Continental?"

"Town Car."

"What color?"

"Black. I always wonder who would want a black Lincoln Town Car. They look like they're either going to a funeral or the airport!" She chuck-led.

"You're right, Lulu," Jakes laughed, "one last thing. Did you happen to catch the license plate of the car?"

She grinned at him, reached into the pocket of her floral housecoat, and came out with a piece of paper. "I wrote it down."

Jakes and I couldn't believe our good fortune. I wanted to stay longer and visit with this wonderful woman but we both knew we had to find this guy. Now. We got up to leave but Lulu stopped us.

"Do you have to go? It's been so nice to talk with you."

I almost cried again. She was lonely. "We'll be back, don't you worry." I took a pen and paper from my pure and wrote down my cell number. As I gave it to her I said, "Here's my number. Give me a call. I'd love to come over and visit and hear more of your stories about the grand days of Hollywood!"

She took the paper and hugged me. I gave her a kiss on her cheek as I thanked her again for saving my life. Jakes even hugged her.

We went out the door and under the archway on the porch. Lulu watched from her window as we walked to Jakes' car. She waved to us as we got in. I felt a little wistful. I guess I missed my mom.

Chapter 48

"Isn't she amazing?" I asked Jakes. "What a life she's had." We were sitting in the front seat of Jakes' car.

"That's a great woman. She wasn't afraid to get involved. Thank God for her." He squeezed my hand in his. "Thank God she's so on top of it that she wrote down his license plate number."

"So now what do we do?"

"I'll get somebody to run the plate," Jakes said.

"Do you think it could be that easy?" I asked.

"Probably not, but it doesn't look like a rental plate. It's got to be registered to somebody."

"What if it's stolen?"

"Could be, but I don't think he'd take the risk of driving around in a stolen car."

"Where are you going, now?" I asked.

"I'll try to find out who the car's registered to."

"Then what?"

"I'll go and talk to the owner. If it happens to be Carver, great. If it's not Carver then maybe it's somebody who knows where Carver is."

"I'll just go with you."

"No," he said, "if I come across this guy I can't have you with me, Alex. I'm gonna have to be able to concentrate completely on him. I can't be worrying about you."

"I can't stay at the hospital forever, Jakes."

He looked at the clock on the dashboard. "It's almost two o'clock. You have to go somewhere else for a few hours. Just till I get a lead on this. Do you feel well enough to drive?"

"Yeah, I feel fine." I thought for a second. "I guess I could go to George and Wayne's place. What about Sarah? She's probably safer not being with me right now."

"You're right. Can she stay with Tonja for a few hours?"

"I'll text her and ask. I'm sure it won't be a problem."

"I'll ask Harry to watch Tonja's place just to be on the safe side." Jakes said. "And I have an idea just to make sure no one follows you."

I sent the text and quickly got a response.

"Okay," I said, reading Tonja's reply. "She says it's fine for Sarah to stay there as long as I need her to."

I dialed George's cell and got his voicemail. "Georgie, it's Alex. Call me ASAP. It's important." I ended the call. "Okay. I guess I'll head back over to the hospital. I want to check on Patti anyway, before I go to George's. So what's the idea to make sure I'm not being followed?"

"Check in with Harry," he said. "Tell him what we found out. Then I want the two of you to switch cars. I'll call him and make sure he's cool with that. I'll follow you over there now just to make sure no one's tailing you."

I kissed him goodbye and lingered close to his face. "Please be careful, okay? Don't do anything stupid." I kissed him again.

"I could say the same thing to you. Once you leave the hospital, go straight to George's and stay put."

Harry was sitting in a chair in front of Patti's room. When he saw me he stood up. "That was pretty fast," he said. "Find him?"

"We found a witness and got a license plate number," I said. "Jakes followed me over here and he's checking out the plate now."

"Yeah," he said, "If he finds him, you shouldn't be there."

"Exactly." I moved to the window and looked at Patti. "Any change?"

"Nope," he said. "Status Quo. You gonna be here awhile?"

"No," I said, "I have to go. Jakes wants me to stay at a friends'—just to be safe. He mentioned something about you driving out to Venice and watching over my neighbor's house. Did he call you about that?"

He nodded and pulled out his car keys from his pocket.

"Yeah. And he wants us to switch cars." He gave me his keys. "The wipers aren't so great, Alex. But it's not supposed to rain until tonight.

Jakes will be back here to take over for me in a couple of hours, and than he wants me to go to your place after that."

"You have my address?" I asked as I handed over my car keys. He nodded. "Thanks so much. You're the greatest. Hey, I can stay long enough for you to take a bathroom break," I said. "Maybe get a cup of coffee?"

"I'll be real quick," he promised. "If you see anybody just start yelling."

"Right." I grimaced.

He hurried down the hallway and then turned back. "Sorry about the mess in my car! I've been meaning to wash it."

"No problem, Harry," I said.

I spent a few minutes watching Patti. My cell vibrated. I walked away from Patti's window and answered it.

"Hey Georgie. Thanks for getting back to me." Even though I was whispering, I was getting the evil eye from a nurse that walked by.

"What's up, Alex? What was the emergency this morning?"

"Long, long story. I can't talk now. I'll tell you everything later. Listen, can I go to your place for a little while?"

"Sure, honey. Are you okay?"

"I'm fine. I just need a place to stay for the evening."

"Wayne's picking me up after work today and we're going to Palm Springs this weekend so the place is all yours. You know where the key is, right?"

"I do. Thank you so much, Georgie. I'll tell you everything. Call me later. Love you."

I walked back to the window and saw that Patti was still unconscious. I sat down to wait for Harry, checking the halls every now and then for a killer.

Chapter 49

Harry wasn't kidding about the mess. There were cardboard coffee cups strewn about his 1998 Camry and a plethora of empty Marlboro packs littered the floor. I even saw an old Dunkin' Donuts box in the back seat. I guess those old cop habits were hard to break after all. Still, I was grateful for the decoy car.

I kept checking the rearview mirror as I made my way down Beverly

Boulevard. George and Wayne had a beautiful old home in Silver Lake, only about twenty minutes from the studio. Even though it wasn't raining at the moment, the constant downpour from the last few weeks had wreaked havoc on the major thoroughfares. I was forced to take side streets to get there. I made a left on Highland and tried to take Franklin towards Silver Lake but it was flooded, too.

I was turning right on Sunset Boulevard when I noticed the dreaded raindrops starting to fall on the windshield. I struggled to find the wipers. When I did, I flipped them on and saw they were pretty useless. Harry wasn't kidding about them either. How did he drive this car in the rain? I turned left on Los Feliz Boulevard and after a few twists and turns pulled into George's driveway. I looked around just to be sure no one had followed me.

It was only three o'clock but clouds were moving in, making the sky dark. From what I could see, no one was behind me. I grabbed for my umbrella and realized I had left it in my car. Maybe Harry had one. No luck. I grabbed the Dunkin Donut box and flattening it out, put it over my head. Snatching my bag, I made a run for the porch, hoping not to get wet. I went to the front door and reached under the mailbox, feeling around for the hide-a-key.

"Got it." I muttered under my breath. I took out the key and opened the door, leaving the donut box on the porch.

I loved their house. Wayne was a brilliant decorator. Hardwood floors, lots of oriental carpets and overstuffed furniture, an abundance of indoor plants and soft lighting. It was the essence of classy, comfortable living.

I dropped my bag on the floor, locked the door behind me. "Now what?" I said to myself shaking off the wet. I figured I better check in with Tonja.

She picked up after a couple of rings. "Hi, Alex. How are you?" she asked.

"I'm good. How's Sarah? You got her, right?"

"Oh, yeah. She's fine. We're just driving back from running some errands. What's going on?"

"Oh, I'm stuck at work for awhile." I lied because I didn't want to get into all the gory details. "Is there any way you can keep Sarah for the evening? I'll get her later, probably around ten or eleven."

Tonja hesitated before answering. "Of course. Are you sure you're alright? You sound kind of stressed."

"I'm fine. Can I speak with Sarah? And Tonja, thanks again. You really are a Godsend."

"Happy to help. I'll put her on speaker. I heard her fumbling with her cell phone for a second.

"Hi, Mommy! Where are you?"

"I'm still working, honey. Tonja's going to watch you tonight, okay? I'll see you later. I love you."

"I love you, too, Mom. I miss you," Sarah said.

"You're at the studio, huh?" Tonja yelled out. Hadn't I just told her that?

"Yes, but I'll be back as soon as I can. Love you, Sarah!" But the connection ended before Sarah could say anything else.

I don't know if it was the rain, or all the drama, but something felt weird to me. I shook it off, chalking it up to the day's events.

I walked around George's house and made sure all the doors and windows were locked. I walked into the kitchen and checked out the fridge. A bottle of Chardonnay looked very tempting but I decided I should keep my wits about me. Besides, Connie's inference to me needing Celebrity Rehab was still echoing in my head. My cell rang but the caller ID said it was a blocked call. Maybe it was Jakes calling from a phone booth somewhere.

"Hello?"

"Hi, Alexis!"

"Mom! Hi. What's going on?"

"That's what I want to know. Where are you? Where's Sarah?" What to say? I couldn't begin to tell my mother everything that had been going on while she was away.

"Sarah's with Tonja, our neighbor. How are . . ."

"But where are you?"

"Uh . . . I'm running late."

"But I see your car out front."

She what? "What do you mean? Where are you?"

"I'm home. I thought I'd surprise you. I saw your car parked on the street. And why is your house such a mess?" Oh no. My mother shouldn't be home alone with Carver and Rockland running around. Thank God Harry was out front. Wait a minute.

"What do you mean the house is a mess? It wasn't when I left this morning."

"All your drawers and cupboards are open and there's stuff all over the floor."

A cold chill went down my spine. "Mom. Are you sure you're alone in the house?"

"Yes. I looked everywhere for you when I got in. Why?"

"A lot's happened while you've been gone."

"You mean Randy's murder, right?"

I was kind of speechless. "Alex? Is something else going on? Did you get involved in something, again? I don't know why I'm even asking. Of course you did."

"Yes, I did. I mean, I am. Before you say anything, let me explain that the man in my car is a good friend of Jakes'. He's watching over Tonja's house while Sarah's there. It's just a precaution, but . . ."

"What man?"

"The man in my car. On the street."

"There's no man in your car. I'm looking at it right now and there's nobody in it."

Where was Harry?

"Maybe he's out checking around the house, or something," I guessed.

"Alex, what is going on? I can't believe you've done this again! Where are you, anyway?"

"I'm at George's. Jakes is looking for a guy . . . I can't get into it right now, it's just better for me to be here for the next couple of hours. Make sure you lock the doors and windows and put the alarm on. I'll be home later tonight. Stay put and I'll call you right back."

I hung up and called Jakes. It went right to voicemail. Then it hit me. I called my mother back on her cell.

"Yes, Alex?" she answered.

"Mom, when you called me before, what phone did you use?"

"The one in the kitchen, why?"

Oh no. My hideout was now officially compromised. I was scrambling, trying to figure out what my next move should be.

"Is Harry back in my car?"

"No. There's no one in your car. Alex, what's happening?"

"I'm not sure, Mom. Stay there and I'll be in touch."

The one thing I did know for sure is I couldn't stay at George's any longer. I grabbed my stuff and ran out the door, locking it behind me. I quickly dashed to Harry's car. I got in and started the engine, calling Jakes at the same time. It went to voicemail.

"Damn! Jakes I need to talk to you! It's an emergency. Call me as soon as you get this." I hung up. "Why the hell isn't he picking up?"

I found out a little later why not, indeed.

Chapter 50

(Jakes)

While I was supposed to be hiding out at George's house Jakes was doing what he could to track down the Town Car Vincent Carver had used when he attacked Patti and me . . .

There were very simple steps to take to do this, but since he was suspended—*suspended,* not on leave like he'd told me—those were steps he couldn't take. So he had to resort to other tactics.

Jakes had a friend who was a P.I. His name was Vail. He'd been in the business a long time, and hated computers. He still did things the old way. Jakes told me when somebody needed brawn they called Slattery, but when they needed brains, it was Vail.

Vail had an office in the Bradbury Building, downtown on Broadway at 3rd Street. Built in 1893 it had been a National Landmark since 1977. These days it housed the Internal Affairs Division of the LAPD. Certain offices were still rented out to private concerns. But the sad thing was the main floor, which had been rented out to retailers, including a Subway sandwich shop.

Jakes' friend Vail had an office in the Bradbury for many years, was one of the holdovers from the old years. When the building was revamped they didn't bother trying to dislodge him.

Jakes opened the door and entered the office of Vail Investigations. There was an ante-room with a desk, but as far as he knew, a girl had never sat there. He walked to the inner office door, which was open. He looked inside, saw Vail at his desk. He knocked.

Vail looked up, sat back in his chair and said, "Cheese-it, the cops!"

"Hello, Dan," Jakes said as he put his cell phone in his pocket.

Dan Vail stood up and approached Jakes with his hand out. "Gotta ask you to turn your phone off." Jakes looked at him quizzically. "Nothin' personal. I just don't trust 'em. Radiation and all."

"I knew you were old school but this is ridiculous, I gotta say, Vail." Jakes chuckled as he turned his phone off.

"Maybe it is, maybe it isn't. Thanks for complying just the same."

Vail was seventy if he was a day, with slate grey hair and a face seemingly made up of cracks. His clothes hung on him like he'd lost a ton of weight, and Jakes hoped it was age, not illness. The handshake was firm, which was a good sign.

"Siddown, kid. What's on your mind?"

"I've got a plate number, Dan," Jakes said. "I need it run down."

"You're kiddin'," Vail said, settling into his squeaky chair. "With all the computers you got at your disposal?"

"Not at my disposal at the moment," Jakes said. "I got suspended."

"No shit?" Vail asked. "Hey, your old man would be proud. You remember what he used to say? Any cop who didn't get suspended at least once wasn't much of a cop."

"Yeah, well, this is my first time and I'm not happy about it. But things still have to get done."

"A plate number, huh?"

Jakes nodded.

"Hand it over, then."

Vail put his hand out. Jakes handed him a piece of paper with a number written on it.

"Whataya want me to do when I find the owner?" Vail asked. "Have a talk with him?"

"No," Jakes said, "I'll do that myself."

"What's this about?" Vail asked.

"You know anything about a killer who wears boots with turquoise tips?"

Vail grinned, showing teeth stained by years of nicotine.

"Carver," he said. "He's a killer."

"For hire?" Jakes asked.

"Used to be," Vail said. "I hear he's in business for himself, these days. Only kills when he has to."

"What kind of business?"

"Makin' money any way he can."

"Like owning a club?"

Vail shrugged. "Maybe."

"Okay, Dan," Jakes said. "Just find out who owns the car, I'll take it from there."

"You think this plate is gonna lead you to Carver?" Vail asked.

"Carver, and more."

"Carver isn't your primary?"

Jakes didn't answer.

"Who are you hopin' he'll lead you to?"

"You don't need to know that, Dan," Jakes said. "And you don't want to."

Jakes stood up, walked to the door, then turned back. "Hey Dan, why don't you open a window in here when you smoke?"

Vail smiled. "You kiddin'? Haven't you heard we're in the middle of 'El Nino'? Besides, I'd get arrested for pollutin' the air outside. This office is the only place I can smoke in peace, anymore."

Jakes laughed. "Take it easy Dan."

"I'll give you a call when I have your information."

"Don't give it to me over the phone," Jakes said. "Just call and invite me to lunch, or for a drink. Okay?"

"You bugged?"

"Maybe."

"Okay, Jakes," Vail said. "Whatever you say."

Chapter 51

The streets of Hollywood were brutal. The roads were full of potholes and crazy California drivers who had no concept of how to drive in the rain. They either went too fast or too slow. I had a nice low level of road rage brewing when I decided to call Jakes again. And again it went right to voicemail. This wasn't like him and it was really starting to piss me off.

"Jakes! Call me as soon as you get this. I'm on my way back to my house. My Mom's home. Call me."

I wanted to call the police, but I wasn't sure who I could trust. I had to get home.

I couldn't see a damn thing as I drove Harry's car down Los Feliz Blvd. The wipers weren't doing much of anything but moving the rivulets of water around and adding to the mess on the windshield. The rain was really coming down and I was trying to move around in the seat to find a spot I could see through. I couldn't keep going on this way or I was going to get killed.

I pulled over, rolled down the window and looked around. Why are there always car rental places on every corner except when you need them? I saw a service station up the road so I drove very carefully about a block and turned into it. With so many gas stations having quick shops instead of mechanics I suppose this was a lucky break.

I could see a pair of legs covered in dirty coveralls sticking out of an old Vega in the garage so I got as close as I could and sprung out of the car, still managing to step into a large puddle.

"Hi, there. Excuse me. I need my wipers replaced," I shouted as I ducked into the cover of the auto shop.

A young Hispanic guy rolled himself out from under the car. He had a dirty wife beater on and was tatted with sleeves. There were so many it was hard to tell what they were, but I could make out one of a rather long blade with blood dripping off of the tip.

"What kind of car you got?" he asked in a heavy street Mexican accent. I noticed a tear drop inked just below the corner of his right eye. I pondered its meaning. Had he been to prison, or did he have a problem with depression?

"Uh, it's a Camry. '98, '99 I think."

"We don't have no wipers for that car." He rolled himself back under the car.

"What am I supposed to do? I can't drive my car in this weather," I said as I looked out at the sheets of rain pelting the pavement. He didn't bother answering me. Probably because he didn't have an answer. Or he just didn't care.

"Shit, shit, shit!!" I said as I ran back to my car and got in. I made another attempt at reaching Jakes with no luck. I had one last option. I looked in my bag making sure I had a script in there. I did. I went back into the garage.

"Hi! Excuse me, sir?" He reluctantly rolled back out from under the car. "My name is Alexis Peterson. What's yours?"

He stood up and walked over to me. He got a little too close. I backed up. "Jesse. My name's Jesse." He smiled, wiping his face with a tattered bandana.

"Hi, Jesse. I was wondering if you have a loaner car I could borrow?"

He smiled. "Does this place look like we have loaners, Mommy?"

"No. It doesn't." He was looking me up and down slowly. I blurted out, "Could I please borrow your car? Look, before you say anything, I'm in the middle of an emergency and I can't see out of my windshield. I have to get home to Venice Beach."

"I don't even know you, why would I do that?" He was looking around my general breast vicinity.

I suddenly realized we were alone and I pulled my jacket around me closer.

"True. I know you don't. And this is going to sound so crazy." I smiled. "But I'm an actress. I'm the star of *The Bare and the Brazen*. Have you ever heard of it?"

He continued to look at me like I was a White Castle hamburger and he hadn't eaten in a week. "I'll prove it to you." I rummaged in my bag and pulled out my script and handed it to him. "See, right there? That's the character I play, Felicia." He looked at me blankly. "Okay so it doesn't ring a bell. Does your Mom watch soaps? Your grandmother is probably a big fan. Anyway, if I can borrow your car just for a few hours, I promise to get it back to you. I will leave you my license and a credit card." He looked from me to the Camry.

"If you're such a big fuckin' star, why do you drive an old Camry, huh?" He smirked.

I sighed. "Look. I will make this worth your while. I have . . ." I pulled out my wallet. ". . . hmm, exactly four hundred and eighty dollars in cash. If you let me take your car, just for the evening, I will give you a total of one thousand dollars. Four hundred and eighty now and the balance when I drop it back off to you."

He looked at me closely. I assumed he was sizing me up and the magnitude of my desperation.

"Make it two grand and you got yourself a car. But I want something else as collateral."

"What kind of collateral?" He looked at the diamond ring on my finger and then at me. He shrugged.

"You're the one who said it was a family emergency, Mommy."

"My mother gave this to me."

He shrugged again and headed back to his rolling thingy.

I looked out at the rain and at the useless wipers. He had me.

"Okay. I'll do it. Here." I took my ring off. He came back over to me and I put it in his hand.

"My car's over there. Be good to her. She's my baby." He was pointing across the way to black Chevy impala with flames painted on the sides. The car was barely an inch off of the ground. It was a classic low rider. Ah, hellllll.

Chapter 52

(Jakes)

Jakes went home to wait for Vail's call.

He arrived in front of his house and saw a car sitting there. As he pulled up beside the car, the driver's side window rolled down. It was Rockland. He put both of his hands on the steering wheel and Jakes noticed Rockland wasn't holding a weapon.

"Rockland," he said. "What the hell are you doing here?"

"Just came to talk, Jakes," Rockland said. "Thought maybe we'd do it inside, in private."

"What, you haven't been inside, already? Maybe leaving me a little present?"

Rockland frowned. "I don't know what you're talking about."

"Yeah, sure," Jakes said. "Okay, come on in. I might have some beer in the frig."

Jakes pulled into his driveway and got out of the car. He wiped the rain from his face. Rockland was waiting for him on the walk, under an umbrella. Jakes gestured him to the door.

Rockland didn't move.

"After you, Detective," Jakes said, waving him up the walk.

Inside, Jakes got two mismatched bottles of beer from the fridge.

"Anchor Steam or Dos Equis?"

"I'll take the Anchor Steam."

"What's on your mind, Sam?" Jakes asked, handing it over.

"You are. You're not doin' yourself any favors, Jakes."

"How so?"

"You're suspended, and you're makin' waves."

"Am I?"

"Come on, Jakes," Rockland said. "You're lettin' that soap opera broad get you all jammed up. Is she worth your career?"

"Like you give a shit. Is she worth yours?"

"Whataya mean?"

"Are we gonna dance around this, Sam?" Jakes asked. "What are you afraid I've found out about you?"

Rockland stared at Jakes, sipped from his bottle.

"What do you think you know?"

"I think you're dirty, Sam," Jakes said. "And I'm gonna prove it."

"Why bother?"

"It'll get you kicked out of the department. Right into a cell."

"You think?"

"Oh, yeah."

Rockland laughed. "You have no idea how things work these days, do you, Jakes?" Rockland asked.

"Why don't you tell me?"

"No," Rockland said, "I don't think I will. I think I'm gonna let you find out for yourself."

Rockland's jacket had gotten hooked on his gun butt, so that the weapon and his holster were showing. Or maybe it wasn't an accident.

Jakes stared at the other man and waited. If Rockland went for his gun, maybe that would be proof enough that he'd commit murder. If he turned and walked out, then he had people do his killing for him. Like Carver.

The relationship between Rockland, Randy and Carver was still unclear. But Jakes knew two things. One of them was a victim, and one was a killer.

What was the other one?

Rockland put his beer down on a nearby table and walked to the front door.

"You'll find out," he said, "the hard way."

"More word games, Sam," Jakes said. "That doesn't help."

Rockland gave him a little wave and walked out.

Jakes went to the front door. He watched Rockland get into his car and drive away. He didn't see anyone else out there watching the house. What was the point of the visit? A warning? Let him know he was in danger of learning the way things ran? Was Rockland telling him he wasn't the only dirty cop involved? Maybe Rockland didn't want to have a fellow cop killed? Was he giving Jakes a chance to walk?

He went to check his messages and realized he never turned his phone back on. When he did, he saw messages from Vail and Alex. He called Vail back.

"Wanna have a drink?" Vail asked.

"That was fast."

"I'm thirsty."

"Where?"

"There's a bar across from the courthouse."

"Are you talking about that dive, 'The Doom Room'?"

"Hey, I'm a cheap date," the private eye said. "Happy Hour starts early there."

"I'll see you in twenty minutes."

They broke the connection. Jakes went to the back of the house to check the windows. Nobody lurking, ready to attack. He stopped in his bedroom, took a .38 in an ankle holster from his closet and strapped it to his right leg. Then he went out the front door, got in his car and drove away.

Chapter 52

It wasn't easy being down here so close to the pavement in the low rider, I felt very vulnerable, like any semi could roll right over and flatten me. At least I had wheels and working windshield wipers. This was Jesse's baby, all right. The interior was pristine. Black leather seats, real wood dash and gear shift. Dice on the rearview mirror and chrome polished like a mirror. I was definitely getting looks from other drivers, but I was concentrating so hard on the wet and slippery road, it didn't matter. I almost jumped out of my skin when my cell rang. I glanced at the caller I.D. It was Jakes. Thank you, God!

"I couldn't reach you. Did you get my message?"

"Yeah. Why are you heading home? You're supposed to be at George's."

"My mom came back early. She called and asked where I was and I told her. She also said that all my drawers and cabinets had been opened and dumped out. Someone was looking for something. Probably the DVDs, don't you think?"

"You're probably right. If someone had been there, it must have been before Harry got there, or he would have seen them. That doesn't tell me why you're not at George's."

"Because after I hung up with my mother I realized she had called me from the house phone."

"Aw, geez. Alright. Head on home. It's good that Harry's out front."

"He's not. My Mom said my car was parked out front but Harry wasn't in it."

"He was probably out looking around the neighborhood."

"It's pouring in Hollywood. If it's raining this hard in Venice, Harry should be anywhere but outside."

"Where are you, Alex?"

"I'm on the ten." I screamed as a big truck drove past me and a blast of water sprayed my car. "Sorry about that. It's a nightmare out here. You're not gonna believe what I'm driving."

"What do you mean what you're driving? You have Harry's car."

"The wipers gave out. I'll fill you in later. Where are you?"

"I'm heading to a meeting. I've got a lead on the Lincoln. Listen. Call your mom and tell her to go to Tonja's. Meet her there and don't leave. Harry's probably back in the car by now. You'll be safe with him out front. I'll call you when I know something."

"Okay. Be careful driving. Love you."

"You, too."

I decided to speed dial Tonja. She picked up after the first ring.

"Hi, Alex."

"Hi there. Just checking in. Are you guys okay?"

"Oh, yeah. Safe and sound at home." There was a brief pause.

"Can I speak with Sarah for a sec?"

"Uh, she's busy playing. But I'll have her call you back, okay?" I was about to tell her that my mother was next door, but she had hung up.

I called my mom next. "He's still not there, Alex. What should I do?"

"Mom, get your stuff and go next door. I just spoke to Tonja and she and Sarah are home, now. I'll be there in half an hour."

"Alex, I can't believe you've gotten into all this foolishness again."

"I know, Mom. Me neither. We'll talk about it later, okay? Bye." I hung up. That's all I needed. On top of Carver and Rockland on my ass and crazy drivers on the road, I needed a lecture from my mother. Even if she was right, I had bigger fish to fry at the moment.

"Whoaaa!" I shouted. I was in the middle of the ten and doing my best to dodge puddles. Suddenly a car swerved into my lane and almost clipped my front bumper. I quickly drove into the lane on my left, narrowly missing another car that was going very slowly. I slammed on my brakes and almost hit the car in front of me. Something slid out from under the front seat and hit my foot. I looked down and saw a gun.

"Oh my God!" I bent down and picked it up, trying my best to keep my eyes on the road, then gingerly placed it on the seat next to me, making sure it wasn't pointed in my direction. My cell rang and I could see from the caller I.D. it was my mother, again.

"Mom! I get it! You're right! I thought I was doing something for Sarah and I realize now—"

"Alex. There's no one home at Tonja's."

"What are you saying? She just called me five minutes ago and said she was home. Mom, are you sure?"

"Yes, I'm positive. No one answered the door, so I looked through the windows and there's nobody home."

"I'll call her." I disconnected with my mom and called Tonja. It went to voicemail. "Hi Tonja. Where are you guys? Call me back."

I could feel it. Something wasn't right. I couldn't put my finger on it. But I knew.

Many things in life depend on how you expect them to make sense. Little things you take for granted.

Harry was probably out canvassing the neighborhood.

Tonja was possibly just out enjoying dinner with my daughter.

Or something was horribly wrong.

Chapter 53

(Jakes)

Jakes walked into "The Doom Room". It was pretty empty except for a couple of guys and one woman at the bar who looked like they were regulars, i.e. alcoholics. Vail was at the end of the bar nursing something dark and munching on something fried.

"Whatta ya have?" The bartender asked Jakes as he moved in front of them.

"I'm good, thanks."

"Suit your self," he said as he went to tend to his regulars.

"So, what have you got for me?"

Vail looked at him and then at his nearly empty glass. "Could we get another of whatever he's having?" Jakes said to the bartender who shot him a dirty look, picked up a bottle of whiskey and began pouring it into a glass.

Jakes shrugged it off, reached into his pocket and put some cash on the bar. Vail looked at the money and then presented a slip of paper with an address on it.

"You sure you don't want me to come with you?" Vail asked, lifting his glass and finishing off the last bit of his drink. "Carver's a bad boy."

"Naw, I've got it, Dan," Jakes said, "but thanks for the offer."

"Whatever."

"What's that you're eating, anyway?" Jakes asked looking at the puffy fried things Vail kept popping in his mouth.

"Pork rinds." Vail replied. "My doctor says these are good for me."

"Seriously?"

Vail shrugged. "That's what he says. Zero carbs, seventeen grams of protein and only nine grams of fat. I figure the whiskey and rinds kind of cancel each other out. Keep the playin' field even, right?"

"Yeah, right."

Jakes got in his car and unfolded the piece of paper Vail had given him. The address was about a fifteen-minute drive from where he was now, in a neighborhood notorious for crime, especially gang activity. The name of the registered owner was Frederick Holder.

Jakes started the car and pulled away from the curb in a driving rain.

There were large homes in among the smaller ones. They had all seen better days, had fallen into different degrees of disrepair. The house he found at the address was putting up at least a token defense against the blight that had overtaken most of the other homes. The yard was cleaner than most, the house two stories of faded dignity, patched and bandaged with some care.

Jakes ran through the downpour, mounted the front porch and rang the bell. The door was opened by a young man in his mid-twenties, munching on a piece of buttered toast.

"Yeah?"

"Fred Holder."

"Fred-er-rick," the boy corrected.

"Well, Fred-er-rick," Jakes said, "I'm looking for a friend of yours."

"Oh? Who's that? I got lots of friends."

"His name is Carver," Jakes said. "Vincent Carver."

The boy stopped chewing.

"I-I don't know anyone by that name."

"That's funny," Jakes said. "The last time he was seen, he was driving your Lincoln."

"My car? Naw. That can't be."

"Where is your car, then?"

The boy licked his lips nervously. He was about twenty-five, hadn't bathed in some time if the funky smell rising up from his pits was any indication. And now there was a new smell. Fear.

"What're you . . . a cop?"

"That's right."

"Lemme see your badge."

"I'm here unofficially."

The boy laughed without humor, tossed his unfinished toast over Jakes' shoulder into the grass.

"The way you're trying to take care of this house, that's a little out of character for you."

"Wait for it," the boy said.

They waited, and a few seconds later a small beagle came trotting over to consume the toast.

"Ah," Jakes said. "You're a nice guy. I get it."

"You're lookin' for Carver unofficially?"

"That's right."

"Does that mean you're not gonna arrest him?"

"That's up to him."

The boy chewed his bottom lip, then backed away and said, "Come on in before somebody sees us."

Jakes stepped inside warily, wishing his .38 was closer than his ankle. But the inside of the house was empty—neat, clean and empty.

Holder led him to a large, spacious living room-spacious because there was very little furniture.

"I've had to hock a lot of it," Holder said, as if reading Jakes' mind. "My father left me this house, but not much else."

"Things are tough all over," Jakes said.

"Yeah, they are."

"That way you got yourself involved with Vince Carver? For money?"

Holder swallowed and said, "Not exactly."

"Fear, then."

Holder didn't answer.

"It's nothing to be ashamed of, Freddy," Jakes said. "Fear is a powerful incentive."

"Yeah, well . . . it's a bitch when you're on the wrong end of it all the time."

"You tell me about Carver, and I'll see to it you don't have to worry about him, anymore."

There was one sofa in the room, and that was it. Holder flopped onto it, gnawed on a fingernail.

"There's no way I can be sure," he said.

"Look, I told you I'm a cop—"

"That don't matter," Holder said. "Carver says—"

"What?" Jakes asked. "Carver says what?"

Holder gnawed the nail so hard he drew blood, but hardly noticed it.

"Oh, I think I get it," Jakes said. "He told you he's got a cop in his pocket."

Holder looked surprised. "How'd you know that?" he asked. "Unless . . ."

"No, son, it's not me," Jakes sad, "but I know who it is, and I want him, too."

"You're gonna take down a cop?"

"I'm gonna take them both down, but I need your help."

"What can I do?"

"Answer some questions."

"That's all?"

"That's it."

Holder thought a moment, then shrugged and said, "Okay."

"How do you know Vince Carver?"

"He knew my dad."

"They were friends?"

"No," Holder said, as if the idea was preposterous.

"Then they had the same kind of relationship that you and Carver do?"

"That's close enough."

"Okay," Jakes said, "let's forget about your father. All I really want to know is, how did Carver get your car?"

"He told me I had to loan it to him."

"Did you take it to him?"

"No."

"Do you know where he is? Where he's staying?"

"No."

"Is he supposed to bring the car back?"

Holder shrugged. "Who knows? He might decide he likes it, and keep it."

"Okay, okay," Jakes said. "You loaned him the car, and he came here to pick it up."

"No."

"What do you mean, no? You just said you didn't bring the car to him."

"I didn't," Holder said. "He had somebody come and pick it up. Why don't you ask her where he is?"

"I will," Jakes said. "Just tell me her name."

"I don't know her last name," Holder said, "only her first."

"Okay, then give me that."

"Toni?" Holder said. "No, maybe it was Tracy . . ."

"Fred."

"I'm tryin'!" Holder said. "She came to the door, said Carver sent her, and then she said her name was . . . Tonja. That was it. Her name was Tonja."

Chapter 54

When my phone rang again it was Jakes.

"Where are you?"

"I'm driving to Tonja's," I said. "My mom went over there and said nobody was home."

"Okay, listen to me," Jakes said, "go to Tonja's but don't get out of the car. Wait for me there."

"She's supposed to be there with Sarah, Jakes!" Even I could hear the edge of panic in my voice.

"Alex, just listen. Don't try to go into her house. Wait for me."

"What is it, Jakes?" I asked. "What's going on?"

"Alex—"

"Tell me!"

He hesitated, then said, "It's Tonja. I found out she's connected to Carver."

"What?"

"I have an informant who says it was a girl named Tonja who picked up that car for Carver."

"How—how can that be? Tonja's my neighbor."

"I don't know. It's too much—it can't be a coincidence."

"Then you're saying Carver may have my daughter?" I pressed my foot down harder on the gas pedal.

"Alex. Don't panic. Don't do anything foolish. When you get to Tonja's wait for me. I'll only be about ten minutes behind you."

I hung up.

I pulled up in front of Tonja's house, screeching my tires. There were no lights inside and that made my stomach drop. I didn't think about giving Jakes' words about waiting for him even a second's consideration before I got out of the car and ran to the front door. I pounded, keeping myself from screaming at the top of my lungs—although I don't know how I did it.

My mother came running up holding a raincoat over her head.

"I found Harry, Alex. He's in the house, now. We think he was drugged. He says Tonja gave him a cup of coffee and that's all he remembers."

"Mom, go back to the house. Stay there, please." I was desperately trying to hold it together.

"What's going on? Where's Sar . . ."

Then I screamed at the top of my lungs. "Please! Go back!"

My mother's mouth opened in shock as she quickly made her way back to our house. She looked almost as terrified as I felt.

I ran around the back of the house trying to find an open door or window. Finally I found a lawn chair and using every fiber of my being, I hoisted it over my head and into the back door window. It crashed through, leaving a huge gaping hole. I reached in and opened the door.

"Sarah! Sarah! It's Mommy." Nothing. I heard myself let out a wail. "Not my baby. Not my baby." I ran through the house, opening closets, looking for anything that might tell me where Sarah was. And then I realized the house was completely furnished as if someone lived there but every closet was practically empty, every drawer the same. It looked like a movie set. I felt like I was in the Twilight Zone. And then I understood why Tonja had never invited me over.

I stumbled down the hallway, ending up in Tonja's bedroom. I threw open the closet and stood there in shock. There was a recording system on the floor. Tonja had been spying on me.

The front door opened with a crash.

"Alex! Where are you?" Jakes yelled.

"Sarah's gone, I have to find her!" I ran into Jakes arms. "We have to find her."

"Oh my God." Jakes had seen the recording equipment.

"Did she ever really live here?"

"I don't know," he said.

I couldn't even guess who had put Tonja in the house to become my neighbor, or why, but this wasn't the time to figure that out.

"Where is she, Jakes? Where's Sarah?"

At that moment my cell phone rang.

"Maybe that's the answer," he said. "Take the call."

"Hello?"

"You want your daughter back?"

"You sonofabitch—"

Jakes cut me off with a wave of his hand. "Put it on speaker," he whispered.

I did.

"Watch your language, Miss Peterson," the voice said. "That's no way to talk to the man who has your Sarah."

I looked at Jakes. He mouthed "Carver" at me. I didn't know if he recognized the voice, or just figured it wasn't Rockland, so it had to be Carver.

"W-what do you want?"

"Well, for one thing I want you to take me off speaker phone. This is just for your ears, not your boyfriend's."

I looked at Jakes and he nodded. I took the phone off speaker.

"All right," I said.

"Good. You've got something I want, Alex," the man said.

"What's that?"

"Some DVDs. We looked around your place and couldn't find them. That is, that dumb bitch Tonja couldn't find them. I assume you watched them."

So Tonja had trashed my house looking for the DVDs.

"What if I did?"

"Then you know why I want them."

"I know why Detective Rockland might want them."

"Yeah," he said, "Sam wants them, too."

"I want my daughter."

"Yeah, I bet you do."

"Is she alright?"

"She's fine."

"Is Tonja taking good care of her?"

"You think you're pretty smart, don't you?"

"No," I said, "I guess I'm pretty dumb, or I wouldn't have been taken in by her."

"Aw, don't feel too bad," he said. "She's a real good actress."

"If you hurt my daughter—"

"I'm not a man who hurts children, Alex," he said. "Now Rockland . . . I can't speak for him."

"What do you want me to do?"

"I'll trade you the DVDs for your little girl."

"When?"

"Tonight. Now."

"Will Rockland be there?"

"Sure. Bring your boyfriend, too. It don't make a difference to me. But if I see any other cops you'll never see your daughter again."

"Where?"

"Come to Randy's house," he said. "We'll make the exchange there."

"Just like that?"

"Why not?" he asked. "I get what I want, and you get what you want."

"I want to talk to my daughter." It was silent for a moment.

"Sure." I could hear him yelling for Tonja. And then.

"Hi, Mommy! Are you getting close?"

I couldn't get my breath I was so relieved to hear her voice. I tried to compose myself as I choked back a sob. "Yes, Baby. I'm close. Are you okay?"

"Yeah. Tonja and I are having fun. We're winning at the game, right Mom?"

"What game, Sweetheart? What game?"

"Tonja said we're playing hide'n seek. Tonja and I are hiding. You and Jakes are seeking." I heard muffled voices.

"Sarah? Sarah?" She was gone.

"Come and get her," Carver said.

I started screaming. "You son of a bitch! You touch one hair on her head and I'll rip your heart out, you piece of shit!"

But he had hung up.

Chapter 55

Jakes ran into my house and grabbed the DVDs from the cupboard I had put them in. I couldn't risk seeing my mother, having her ask me to explain what was going on. Jakes told her and Harry that we had everything under control—which couldn't be further from the truth.

"I don't understand," I said, as Jakes drove his car. "Why would Carver say it's okay to bring you?"

"Because then we're all in one place," Jakes said. "Carver and Rockland want to finish this all at one time. Nice and neat."

"How are we going to do it, Jakes? How?"

"Believe me," he said, "I'm thinking about it."

"Maybe this'll help."

I took the gun out of my purse, the one that had slid out from under the seat of the car I was driving.

"Holy crap," he said. "Where'd you get that?"

I told him.

"Who'd you borrow that car from? A gang banger?"

"A mechanic."

"A hit man?"

"A car mechanic," I said. "Although he looked a bit like a banger. Why?"

"That's a Glock," he said. "Cops *and* bangers are carrying them, these days."

"Well, here," I said, holding it out to him.

He took it and tucked it into his belt.

"I have one for you." he reached down to his ankle and came up with a gun I recognized as a revolver. "It's my off duty gun, a thirty-eight. Take it."

I did.

"Put it in your bag. All you have to do is point and pull the trigger. Can you do that?"

"If it means saving Sarah, hell yes."

"Let's hope you won't have to."

He turned his attention to his driving. The rain was coming down hard again; the inside of the car smelled damp. Our clothes were soaked.

"Thought of anything yet, Jakes?"

"We're gonna get Sarah back, and take those bastards down, Alex," he said. "That's what we're gonna do."

"But how?" I needed something concrete to hold onto before I lost it completely.

"I'll know by the time we get there." He reached for my hand. "Take some deep breaths, Alex. It's gonna be okay." I looked from him to the rain outside, praying he was right.

We were within a block of Randy's house when Jakes pulled over to the curb and stopped.

"What are you doing?"

"Hit the redial on your phone," he said. "We want to hear Sarah's voice again to make sure she's there."

I hit the redial.

"Where are you?" Carver demanded.

"On the way, but I want to talk to Sarah."

"Forget it."

"How do I know she's okay?"

"Okay, okay," he said, annoyed, "just hold on. I'll get 'er."

I looked at Jakes and nodded.

"Okay," Carver said, "you get to hear a few words. That's all."

"But—"

"Hi, Mommy," Sarah said, "me and Tonja are still hidin' from you—"

"Oh, Honey, are you—" but she was gone.

"Okay," Carver said, "you heard her. Now get over here."

The line went dead, and I couldn't stop the tears.

"How did she sound?" Jakes asked

"Fine. She thinks we're playing a game, that she and Tonja are hiding from us."

"Okay," he said, "at least she's not scared. That's something."

"Oh God oh God, Jakes. What if . . ."

"Not gonna happen. We're getting our girl back. She's gonna be okay."

He gave me a quick, firm hug and then started the car again.

"Ready?" he asked, pulling away from the curb, "let's get this over with."

I turned and looked at the DVDs on the back seat, There were two. I had hid them in plain sight, in a cupboard, inside the movie DVD boxes, along with Sarah's other animated films. Obviously while Tonja had blown through my house looking for them she hadn't used much imagination.

One of the DVDs would be of interest to Carver, but the second was just one we picked at random. Jakes said we had to hold one back, because Carver and maybe Rockland were going to try to take us and the DVDs without setting Sarah free. We needed an ace in the hole. Jakes had hidden it as well as he could, in the trunk of the car. He said somebody would have to take the car apart to find it.

When we reached the house, there was an absolute deluge happening, with strong wind. This was the kind of downpour that caused flooding, and landslides.

The lights were on in Randy's house.

"Okay," Jakes said, "Let's go."

"But—we don't know what we're doing."

"We're getting Sarah back," he said, looking at me. "No matter what happens, that's number one. Understand?"

I nodded.

"So we'll go in there and make the trade, and see what happens."

We got out of the car, my heart pounding, the .38 he'd given me heavy in my purse. Would I be able to shoot someone, even to save Sarah? We were going to find out.

Chapter 56

We were soaked through and through by the time we got to the front door, which was ajar.

"Let me go first," Jakes said. With his gun in his hand he pushed the door open and entered. I followed. It was warm in the house, and all the lights seemed to be on.

"Carver?" Jakes yelled.

"In here," a man's voice called back. "Just keep comin'."

We kept moving down the hall until we came to the large living room. In the center of it stood Carver. He was alone.

"Where's my daughter?" I asked.

"She's fine." Carver said.

"I want to see her. Please."

"You bring the DVDs?" he asked.

I held up the DVDs. What were the chances he'd want to check them before we made the exchange?

"Walk down the hall. Both of you, slowly."

He had a gun on Jakes and me as we headed down the hallway. He stopped in front of Sarah's room and opened the door a crack.

Sarah was on the floor playing with some of her Barbie's Randy had gotten for her. Tonja looked up at me from where she was sitting next to Sarah and gave me a defiant look.

"Hi, Mommy. You found us!" She jumped up and we hugged each other.

"Hello, Sweetie, are you okay?"

"I'm fine," she said, with a shrug, "I've been playing in my room with Tonja. It makes me miss Daddy, though. Being here."

I put her hair behind her ears and kissed her. "I'm sure it does, Honey," I said. "We'll be going home soon, don't worry."

"Yeah, we'll all be going home soon," Carver said. "Let's go." He pulled me out of the room.

"I'll see you in a minute, Sarah!" I yelled out as he closed the door. He pushed us back into the living room.

"Mommy!" I heard her yell, and for the first time she sounded scared.

There was no doubt about who he was. He was the man I'd seen stab Patti. He was the man with the blue-tipped cowboy boots. He had a cadaverously thin face and long, lifeless brown hair that hung past his shoulders. This time he was wearing his cowboy hat, again.

Jakes had his gun down by his leg, where Sarah hadn't been able to see it. I didn't see a gun in Carver's hand. I looked around but there was no sign of Rockland.

"It's obvious Tonja trashed my house trying to find these," I said. "But why did she become my neighbor?"

"That was easy," Carver said. "Rockland found out the house down the street from you was available, so we rented it for Tonja."

"To keep track of me through Alex?" Jakes asked.

Carver laughed. "You have a big opinion of yourself, Jakes. No, we wanted to keep track of Randy."

"Through me?" I asked. "I had nothing to do with Randy."

"Yeah, well," Carver said, "Rockland didn't know that. He said ex-wives and husbands were always connected. Guess he was wrong. You two hardly ever saw each other—that is, until he filed for custody."

"Wait," I said, "you, Randy, Rockland, you were partners?"

"We bought that club together," Carver said, "and we all used phony names. It was supposed to be the first of many joint ventures. Randy was using money from his various investors, Rockland used his police contacts and knowledge to get us cheaper prices, and I . . . well, I was supposed to be some kind of . . . enforcer. But I was too smart for that."

"Rockland used his position to force sellers to sell at low prices?" Jakes asked.

Carver shrugged. "Everybody has skeletons, you know. Your colleague was really good at finding them."

"But you," Jakes said, "you found his, didn't you? You were blackmailing him with these DVDs."

"And Randy," I said. "You were blackmailing him?"

"Randy, your precious daughter's father, was even more bent than we were."

"He stole," I said, "but he didn't kill. You killed him."

"Rockland killed him," Carver said.

"Giving you more to hold over his head," Jakes said.

"Enough background. Bring those DVDs over to me," Carver said.

"No way," Jakes said. "We get Sarah first."

"That ain't the way it's gonna work, Detective," Carver said.

"Then send Sarah over and I'll bring you the DVDs at the same time," Jakes said.

Carver gave it some thought, then said, "No, I want Alex to bring them to me."

"No way," Jakes said, again. "Then I'll have Sarah but you'll have Alex."

Carver looked at me. "Why don't we let the lady decide?"

"I'll take them to him," I said.

"Alex—"

"Just get her out of here, Jakes."

"And put your gun away, Dude," Carver said. "Your hands should be empty to take that little girl."

Jakes didn't move.

"Put it away," Carver said to Jakes, and suddenly his gun was in his hand. "Hey, I'm not even askin' you to drop it."

Reluctantly, Jakes stuck the gun into his belt.

"Okay," Carver said, "Alex, bring me those DVDs."

"Give us Sarah, first"

"We'll go down the hall and get her as soon as I have the DVDs in my hand."

He didn't say he wanted to check them, just that he wanted to hold them. I walked over and handed the two DVDs to him.

"Now I want Sarah—" I said, backing away.

"Hold on," Carver said. "You two may think I'm stupid, but I ain't. I'm willin' to bet that at least one of these is bogus."

Jakes and I didn't move, or say anything.

"I think I'll keep both these ladies," Carver said to Jakes, pointing his gun at me, "and you go and get me the real DVD."

"What do you care about the DVDs?" Jakes asked. "They implicate Rockland, not you."

"Which means he'd pay me a lot of money for 'em."

"On a cop's salary?"

Carver laughed. "You ain't looked at your buddy Rockland's finances, lately," he said. "He's turned that badge into a lot of money over the years."

"So why'd Rockland have you kill Randy?" Jakes asked.

"You got that wrong, Dude," Carver said. "Sure, I did some wet work for Rockland, but I didn't kill Randy. I told you. That was your colleague. He graduated from shady real estate deals to murder."

"So you're saying Rockland's the killer," Jakes said.

I wondered if Sarah could hear us discussing her father's murder from behind the closed door of her room.

My purse was slung over my shoulder, hanging down around my waist. I wondered if I could get the gun out without Carver realizing what I was doing.

"He's the man you want," Carver said.

"And why would you be telling me that if you're plannin' on squeezing some money out of him?"

Carver grinned and shrugged. "I guess maybe I got somethin' planned, huh?" He gestured at me with his gun. "Now you go and get me that last DVD."

"Wait a minute," Jakes said. "If you're not the killer, then you'd be a fool to kill anybody right now."

"You think I wouldn't kill your girl here if you don't bring that DVD back to me? Is that what you're sayin'?"

I saw from the look on Jakes' face that he thought he might have pushed Carver too far. I knew he'd kill me, because I saw him stab Patti.

"Okay, wait—" Jakes said.

"Maybe I should make an example of one of these girls, huh?" he asked. "Maybe I should bring Tonja out and put a bullet in her right in front of the little girl. She's a stupid bitch, anyway. She wasn't supposed to leave you alone in the club that night, but the dumb bitch got excited . . . okay, never mind. Maybe I'll just put a bullet in somebody." The gun wavered. "Who should it be?"

"Carver," Jakes said, "don't do anything stupid."

"You ready to get me that DVD?" Carver asked.

I slid my hand into my purse and closed my fingers tightly around the gun.

Chapter 57

My fear was that once there was shooting, Sarah would hear and be frightened. She might even come running out of the room. But there was no way

I intended to leave—or have Jakes leave—without her. Still, my hand just would not come out of my purse.

"Carver! Hold it!"

We all looked at the man who had stepped through the doorway from another bedroom. It was Detective Sam Rockland, and he had a gun in his hand, pointed at Carver.

"Sam," Carver said, "you were supposed to stay in that room."

"I'm not gonna stay in there while you kill people," Rockland said. "And I sure as hell ain't gonna stay in there while you try to pin a murder on me."

"This was supposed to be *my* show, Detective," Carver said. He was still pointing his gun at me. "They're supposed to believe everything I say, not what you feed 'em."

"Well, I don't like the way you're runnin' it," Rockland said. "Jakes, get your girls out of here."

"Sam—"

"And take Tonja, too. She's just a stupid bitch who does whatever Carver tells her to do"

"Jakes," Carver said, "don't you move. Sam, are you crazy? We need those DVDs."

"What makes you think we don't already have 'em?" Rockland asked.

"Like I said," Carver replied, "I ain't stupid. Neither are these people. They wouldn't walk in here with everything I want, and trust me to give 'em back the kid. Hell, I wouldn't trust me to do that."

"Look," Rockland said, "I was willing to set Tonja up to watch Alex. But we never said anything about kidnapping her daughter."

"Well, things got complicated, didn't they?" Carver pointed the gun at Rockland. "And they're about to get even more complicated."

I kept my eyes on Jakes, waiting for him to pull the gun from his belt, almost hoping that he wouldn't. Maybe these guys would shoot each other and save us all a lot of trouble.

He met my eyes, then looked at my hand in my purse and shook his head slightly. He didn't want me to take it out.

"Rockland, don't be a fool. You're makin' this harder than it should be."

"No, Carver," Rockland said, "I've *been* makin' it harder than it should be, but not anymore. Put down your gun. You're under arrest."

"What?"

"You heard me."

"Now?" Carver said, incredulously. "You're actin' like a cop now?"

"It's what I should've done a long time ago, when you first told me you killed Randy."

"Shut up!" Carver yelled. "Damn it, Sam—" And he fired.

The bullet struck Rockland in the chest. A look of pure surprise came over his face. He slumped against the door frame, then slid down to a seated position on the floor. The gun dropped from his hand.

Across from us Jakes had drawn his gun and was pointing it at Carver, who had taken a quick step toward me and grabbed my arm. He pulled me in front of him. I could feel his gun in my ribs. My heart was beating hard enough to jump out of my chest.

"Put it down, Carver."

"Now you know I'm serious," Carver said. "Now you know I'll kill 'er."

"I'm not lettin' you out of here, Carver," Jakes said.

"I'm leavin', Jakes, and I'm takin' Alex with me. I'll call and tell you where to meet me with the last DVD."

"You've got all of them in your hand," Jakes said. "Let her go."

"Naw," Carver said, "I don't buy it."

"And what good is hidin' them now?" Jakes asked. "They don't incriminate you, but killin' Rockland right in front of witnesses sure does."

I could feel Carver's mind working.

"We're gettin' out of here," he said, backing up toward a sliding glass door behind us.

"Carver—" Jakes said, warningly.

"We start shootin' in here that little girl might get hurt, Jakes," Carver said, still dragging me back to the door.

"It's over, Carver! You can't kill everybody."

"Then I'll just have to settle for killin' Alex, won't I?"

"Damn it—" Jakes said.

We reached the door. Both of Carver's hands were full—one with the gun, and one with me—so he said to me, "Open it."

"No."

"I'll start shootin' and your daughter will come runnin' down the hall. A bullet might even hit her," he said in my ear. "Open it."

I reached behind us, found the lock, flicked it and slid the glass door open. The rain and wind came rushing in, but Carver pulled me outside.

Chapter 58

Jakes told me later that he rushed to Rockland's side. The detective was still breathing, but it was labored and his color was bad.

"Sam—"

"Get Carver . . ." was all he said before he passed out.

Jakes ran to the sliding door, gun in his hand and dashed out into the storm . . .

We were in the back yard, part of which had already slid down the mountain with Randy. The wind was whipping us around, the rain stung like tiny little needles. Now that Sarah wasn't within range I started to struggle.

"Stop fightin' me, bitch!" Carver said.

We were in the center of the yard and he was looking for a way out. Actually, it used to be the center of the yard. Since part of it had fallen away in an earlier storm we were now closer to the edge. If we went over, we'd fall a lot further than Randy had. Because of all the erosion, it was now a sheer drop to the Pacific Coast Highway.

"Carver!" I heard Jakes yell, but I could hardly see him. And if I couldn't see him, that meant he couldn't see us. And if he couldn't see us, he couldn't save me, and he was so supposed to save me.

"Jakes. Jakes, over here!"

"I'll kill him!" Carver shouted to me.

Some of his long hair was whipping around in the wind. The rest was plastered to his head. His hat was long gone. I tried to pull out of his grasp.

"Bitch," he shouted, again.

I was getting tired of being called that.

"Alex!" Jakes was closer.

Carver raised his gun and fired. I didn't know if he could see Jakes, or if he was firing wildly. Either way, he might hit him. I stomped on his instep and he flung me to the ground angrily.

"Stop. Calling. Me. Bitch." I pulled up my legs and kicked him with all the force I could muster.

He staggered backwards, then he was falling. His arms waved crazily as if he was trying to fly.

I reached out to grab him but it was too late.

Carver was gone . . .

I felt Jakes' strong arms grab me and drag me to my feet. He hugged me tightly, then pulled me back to the house. We went back in through the sliding glass door and closed it. Tonja was standing in the middle of the living room.

"Where's my daughter?" I demanded.

"She's still in her room," she answered, a slight look of regret on her face. "Look, Alex, I never would have let anything happen to her." She shrugged. "Times are tough. I needed the money."

I looked at her with utter contempt.

"Vincent?" Tonja asked as Jakes handcuffed her to a door.

"He's gone," Jakes said. "He went over the cliff." Then Jakes walked across the room to check on Rockland, but he was dead.

"I better call this in," he said. "I'll have a lot of explaining to do."

I started toward the bedroom to get Sarah. As I walked past Tonja I stopped to look at her. Then I surprised myself when I hauled off and punched her right in the face. She went down so loosely I knew I had knocked her out. Cold. She was lying on the floor, one arm hanging from the cuffed doorknob, looking like a broken doll.

I opened the bedroom door to find Sarah on the floor. She was still playing with her Barbies. I ran to her and scooped her up in my arms.

"Hi, Baby! You okay?" I hugged her tightly.

"Yeah, Mommy."

"Oh, Sweetie, I'm so, so glad."

"I'm sad about Daddy."

"I know you're sad about your Dad, Honey, but you know you always have me. Forever and ever, right?"

Jakes walked in and sat down on the floor next to us.

"And Jakes, too, right?" Sarah asked, reaching her little arms out to him. "We have Jakes, too, forever and ever?"

Jakes looked at me, questioning with his eyes.

I smiled and slowly nodded to him.

"Yes, Sarah. You have me forever and ever, too," he said.

He wrapped his arms around both of us. I looked at him with tears in my eyes and kissed him tenderly on the lips.

"Mommy, that's gross!"

We sat there crying and laughing until the squad cars pulled up in front of the house.